CONNECTED

Mob Stories From My Past

A NOVEL BY

JOE FERRY

Edited By Phil Moffa

CONNECTED

Mob Stories From My Past

A Novel By Dr. Joe Ferry

Edited By Phil Moffa

Illustrations & Layout By Greg MacAvoy

Proofreader: Patrick MacAvoy, Esq.

Second Proofreader: Alison Ferry

Cover Art By Cuda Vendetta

Worldwide Publication

By Dr. Joe Ferry

www.joeferrymusic.com

joeferrymusic@gmail.com

Available in Electronic & Paper Copy

My love & thanks to:

My wife Alison, My Family, Alan Piciocchi, Tommy Salera, Uncle Bean, Phil Moffa, Jay Mumford, Cuda Vendetta, Patrick MacAvoy, Greg MacAvoy, Glasschord Magazine, Tom Schwarz, Xander Zimmer, Delia Drumm, Dana Mancuso, Alana Rose, Bill Junor, John Delate, Shontay Richardson, Lily Thrall, Dan Hanessian, Peter Denenberg, Nick Patrissi, Charlie B. Dahan, Randall Grass, Kevin Byrne, Doug Munro, Bill Guerrero, and Tommy McDonnell.

Always In My Heart, Always On My Mind, Always Alive In My Soul:
Family & Friends Who Have Gone Home To The Lord

For My Father,

Tony Ferry

Connected

CONNECTED

Prologue

(Connected: For My Father)

My mom always said that I was *Trouble,* almost from birth. The nickname took. So that's what you can call me. For as long as I can remember, the two things I enjoyed doing most were walking and stealing. The first thing I stole was a ceramic duck from the front lawn of my Uncle Zoot's house. He is my Godfather and he got the biggest kick out of it when Dad and he found the lawn ornament in the back seat of our car. Uncle Zoot said to Dad, "You're teaching him well, Breezie." I was four years old.

Walking is something that I still find therapeutic, although stealing has fallen off my list of favorite things to do. I recall walking throughout our neighborhood in the city. I especially enjoyed walking late at night when everyone was asleep, the apartment buildings dark and the streets quiet. It was then that I did my thinking, my meditating. I made decisions that impacted my life profoundly as I walked. I made decisions that impacted the lives of others as well, for better and for worse. It was then that I dreamed up my nefarious schemes, it was then that I spoke to God and it is as I walk that I speak to my dad now. Our minds, so in tune all our lives, remain so even though my dad can barely think now. The hearts of our brains are connected. Our heartbeats are in sync. It is as I walk that I hear him the loudest and clearest. As I walk, it is as if he were walking beside me again. As I walk, the years roll back and that fearsome, vicious, witty, generous man, my father, is in his prime again. *"We are suited to our callings, boy. Make no excuses for yourself. We are complex creatures. We are shadows and light. Good and bad."* I have based my life on this premise. I have heeded my dad's words of street wisdom. I cannot help but be who I am. But now I hear Dad saying, "My time is almost up. I'm tired of this life." I know that he will not be around much longer. Oddly, I am not sad. I do not cry. I know that as long as I walk, whether in New York City among the skyscrapers or in the rural countryside where I now live, my dad will walk with me. Wherever I am, my dad is with me. His heart is my heart. We are, in so many ways, the same person. I feel his rage, I feel his joy, I feel his generosity, I feel his ferocity, I feel his brutality and I feel his humanity. I will not wear black gloves at his funeral. I will walk beside his coffin so I can hear him clearly. I will touch his coffin with my bare hand and I will feel our spirits breathe in harmony. I will hear him say, as I have heard him say to me time and again, *"We will always be connected, my son."* Nothing will break that connection. Ever.

Sister Maria's Titties

I remember the first time I ever saw a woman's titties. I was nine years old and in grammar school. I went to Catholic elementary school and high school so my teachers were nuns, brothers and priests until I was at university. I was in puppy love with Sister Maria. She was my fourth grade teacher. She was kind, sweet, caring and beautiful. I didn't know about tits at that point in my life. I was too young. I had not yet begun to hang with my father and the call girls he hired to entertain at the parties in *The Little Shop of Insanity*. I was interested in the New York Yankees and playing my bass. That was it. My violent streak hadn't really even begun to blossom yet, although it was beginning to rear its ugly head. I punched my cousin Gloria in the stomach simply because she said, "Hey, Trouble, how are you?" Something about the way she said it rubbed me the wrong way. So I knocked her on her ass. Looking back, I was a little monster. I don't know how my mom put up with me. But while I had the makings of a mob guy at the tender age of nine, I still didn't know women had breasts. Sister Maria changed that.

One Friday afternoon in May 1959 as we were leaving school, a gust of wind caught Sister Maria's smock. The nuns back then wore black habits with big white bibs that covered their chests. As the wind swept under the good Sister's bib, it blew linen cloth up over her face. There, for about three glorious seconds, bounced the first, most perfect titties I had ever seen in my life. *Holy Fucking Shit!* My little hairless pecker did a Tarantella. *What on*

God's earth are those things? I was in love with Sister Maria's boobs. All I wanted was to smother myself in them. That three-second snapshot etched itself onto my temporal lobe where it remains today. Sister Maria could not have been more than 19 years old. She had big blue eyes and gorgeous, smooth skin. Her titties were perfection, truly heavenly. I thought to myself:

God, you outdid yourself!

There could not be more superb titties in all of creation.

The girls with whom I went to school at that point had *no* boobs. Some of the guys had bigger boobs than most of the girls. I was not used to seeing such magnificent things on a female. *Freddie The Fat Fuck*, as we called my pal Fred Spampanino, had huge boobs. They were sagging, hideous sacks. But Sister Maria was another story. *Lord Have Mercy!*

I thought, *"If Sister Maria has such luscious boobs, maybe some of the other nuns do too."* I didn't realize that *all* women had boobs. I thought just *nuns* had boobs. I thought perhaps it had something to do with being a nun. God gave you boobs. The thought never occurred to me that maybe it's a *woman* thing. So I tried to check out the other nuns. This was a bad idea. First of all, there were no other 19-year old nuns at my school. They were all over 100 years old with warts and bad breath. Plus Freddie's boobs were bigger than theirs. Secondly, they were mean bitches. They were cruel and violent. They beat the shit out of most of us. The nuns never hit me. I don't know why. I kept to myself and did my work. *I wasn't looking for strife in my life*. But some of my friends got serious beatings. When a nun beat up a kid, she would sneer, *"Don't you DARE tell your parents or tomorrow you'll be sorry you were ever born!"* These were supposed to be the wives of God. I could see God getting hitched to Sister Maria. *I wanted to marry her!* But, *damn*, what was He thinking with these other hags, these fucking wicked witches? We were petrified of further physical abuse so we told our parents that we got hurt playing touch football in the street. Our parents bought it because we were always getting hurt in such ways anyway. I look back now and, while I still would never wish harm on a Holy person, I am appalled by the things those nuns did to a bunch of grade school children. They beat up the girls as well. *That* shocked and scared me even more than seeing Freddie get slapped around. I knew Freddie could take it. He was a bull. But it was horrifying to see one of the girls getting beaten. They were wisps. The nuns would beat them until the girls' knees buckled. It was a fucking shame. I have no doubt that it influenced and furthered my violent tendencies.

I never saw Sister Maria's tits again, just that one time. After grammar school I went to a boys high school. A lot of those guys had big boobs too. It was a riot in the shower after gym class. But my pecker didn't do the Tarantella. That did not happen until my 16th birthday, when Dad bought me a whore. My dick was a dancing fool that night. When she put it in her mouth for the first time, I didn't know what was happening. I thought, "*What the fuck is this bat shit crazy bitch doing? Is she going to bite me? I will not like that!*" But she surprised me and I thought, *"Well, I can get used to this!"*

You know, even as this stunning woman, this professional call girl, sucked my dick and caressed it with her tongue, I could not get the good nun out of my mind. The image of my dear Sister Maria's tits was still etched onto my temporal lobe.

In my mind, as I turned 16 on that night so many years ago, Dad's birthday present was wearing a nun's habit.

Otto The Corpse

Kids are stupid, inconsiderate, mean little jerk-offs. When we grow to adulthood, we mature emotionally to realize, hopefully, how much damage we have done and perhaps change our ways. We realize that love is the key. Of course by then a Girl Scout could kick our ass, so naturally we see the light.

One of my earliest assaults on humanity occurred when I was 12, in 1962. My friends and I loved to play football and our favorite field was the side yard of this geezer's house. He lived down the block from me. His lawn was beautiful, mowed and manicured. It was level, too, a level playing field. It was perfect. The geezer's name was Otto. Needless to say, he was not very happy with a gang of snot-nosed punks in cleats tearing his magnificent lawn to shreds. He'd come charging out the side door of the house, snorting like a bull and swinging his leather belt like a maniac. We'd scatter. Game over. Otto would be left standing alone, panting. You'd think we'd learn to go to the park, where they had an actual football field with goal posts and everything. Nope. Otto's side yard was our home field and that's where we held our weekly games. We'd never heard the term "trespassing". As I said, kids are stupid. Time after time, we'd get a game going and time after time, Otto, tall, lanky, and silver-haired, would come blasting out of the house. He could not catch us, much as he tried. He'd swing that belt of his, fumbling like a broken-down, ungainly, drunken samurai warrior in baggy pants. He'd hit himself with the belt as we ran circles around him. It was pitiful. Then, in a flash, we'd vanish, wise guy ghosts. Otto would be left huffing and puffing, his pants hanging around his ass, mumbling, "Fucking piss ants." It was fun.

One day, during one such outing, we harassed Otto like a swarm of psychotic killer bees buzzing around a honey-coated scarecrow. Suddenly, as we jeered and laughed, he clutched his chest and keeled over. Civic-minded, good kids we were *NOT*. The fun was over. Otto seemed to be having a seizure of some sort. This did not concern us. So we left him in his yard on the ground, struggling for breath, and we walked up to the candy store, where we drank Cokes and ate salt pretzels. As the wonderfully addictive drink cooled off our parched throats and the yummy salt pretzels filled our hungry bellies, Otto died where we left him. By the time we finished our snack and walked back to Otto's for another game, the ambulance guys were loading him into a body bag. We didn't give a shit; it wasn't our fault. He should have taken better care of himself. He smoked and drank too much. We didn't care. At least that's what we told ourselves.

Now, a little known fact about my friends and me is that we were altar boys. We saw no problem terrorizing Otto on Saturday and serving Holy Mass on Sunday. Even though it was a bit scary to serve as altar boys - the motionless yet seemingly mobile statues, the smell of the incense, the elaborate garb of priests and the Latin that was chanted in hushed tones - it paid us $5 each per Mass. Righteous bucks. We did two or three Masses a day at times. I was rolling in money. We served Mass on weekdays as well. There was an extra perk to that: we got out of school in the mornings. But while the money and perks were great, the aforementioned eerie vibe was a bit too much for us to handle. So we did what any wise guy in our situation would do, we rolled a fatty out back and smoked ourselves into oblivion. We'd float through Mass in a ritualistic fog then collect our cash and dash. It was beautiful, until the Otto thing caught up with us. A couple of days after the geezer died, I glanced at the schedule on the bulletin board in the church office. My cousin, Antonio, and I were listed to serve Otto's funeral. This was not good. Funerals were difficult enough to do when we didn't know the stiff. You had to shake the incense holder over the coffin and say Latin words, the meanings of which we knew not. We'd brush against the coffin and it made our skin crawl, stoned as we were. But knowing that the coffin would contain the remains of Otto, whom we had so merrily taunted for so long, scared the hell out of us. So we came up with an idea. No, we did not ask to be replaced for Otto's funeral. That would have been the logical thing to do. Of course, if we were logical we wouldn't be in our current fix. No! Our idea was much better: lace our usual morning bracer, Acapulco Gold, with opium! Yes, that was the only route to take and that is what we did. We had a friend, Joe "Corvette", who was our connection. Joe drove a candy-apple-red 1959 Corvette that he would occasionally let us drive, although not when we were high. He hooked us up with the main ingredient that would make this scary situation bearable.

The next morning before Otto's funeral started, we blazed a fire of extraordinary blend and immediately left planet Earth. As we walked behind the priest to the front of the altar, the marble floor turned to Jell-O. I could feel it squishing in my socks. We looked out and saw a church full of people. Wow! We didn't think Otto had any relatives, let alone friends, who gave a shit about him. But there they were. Some were crying. Paranoia set in. They must know we killed him!!! The statues came to life, turned their heads and growled at us in low, guttural tones, "Bad boys." The heads of the people in church inflated and deflated, like balloons, with each breath I took. I could hear Otto The Corpse calling to us from within his coffin, *"Fucking piss ants."* Oh man, this was bad. Just then, an idea occurred to me in a brilliant flash: *Let's ask Father Vito to replace us for Otto's funeral.* Then I realized that the funeral had begun and we were serving it. *DAMN!!! When shit goes wrong...* Now it was time for us to do the thing with the incense. My legs turned into Slinky-like springs and I couldn't stand still. I tried not to approach the coffin but my Slinky legs moved with a will of their own. I stood beside the coffin of Otto The Corpse. It was zero hour. As I did the incense thing and recited the Latin words, I noticed five boney fingers pushing the lid of the coffin open. *WHAT THE FUCK?* I almost puked. Soon, Otto The Corpse had pushed the lid all the way open and he sat up in his coffin. Now my legs turned into pillars of stone. I couldn't move. I couldn't run. *OTTO, YOU TOOK US SERIOUSLY? WE WERE ONLY KIDDING WITH YOU.* Otto The Corpse turned his head, which creaked on his shoulders, his eyes bulging, and he screamed, *"I'm finally gonna get you, fucking piss ant!"* He reached for his belt, and I braced myself for the thrashing I deserved. But Otto hesitated as he *felt for the belt*. He was in one of those split lid coffins so most of his body was covered. It was then that we both realized he wasn't wearing a belt. He wasn't even wearing pants! He wore only a shirt, tie and jacket. He was a corpse. Corpses don't need belts or pants. Once again, I had flirted with disaster and came through smelling like a rose. *"Lie back down in that coffin, you drunk, you cannot catch me," I gloated. AND HE DID!!!* He pulled the lid back down over himself and I heard Father Vito say, "The Mass is ended. Go in peace." The funeral directors wheeled Otto The Corpse out of the church, put his sorry ass into the hearse, drove him to the cemetery and buried him. He lies there still.

Some guy bought Otto's house and covered that magnificent lawn with cement. He also built a barbecue pit and installed an inground swimming pool. He had a really cute daughter, 12 years old, same age as me. She took a liking to me and would invite me to the house for cookouts and to go swimming. After a while, her pop, a pretty cool guy, would go inside and we were all alone. I'd lie back on a lounge, sipping lemonade with the cutest babe in the neighborhood. Occasionally, as I gazed at the cement slab that was once a lavish lawn so lovingly nurtured by poor Otto, it struck me how life changes. I would recall the fun we had taunting and harassing Otto as we tore muddy holes into the grass with our cleats. Those were the days. To top it off, I was chilling on his former property, with the consent of the owner, and the owner's daughter was serving me lemonade. Sometimes, when it got dark out, she even let me touch her titties. All the while Otto The Corpse was rotting in his grave.

Hercules

I was a vicious little bastard. I guess it comes from the influence of my surroundings. My home life wasn't violent. We had a loving home. However, I stepped into the middle of a war zone once I left the house. The nuns and priests beat us in school, there was always a wise guy looking for a fight and I lived in Mob Central. On the one hand, I was usually afraid of my own shadow, quiet, peace loving, respectful, and shy. On the other hand, if pushed, I had no compunction whatsoever to try to kill you. Arthur MacArthur pissed me off one day when I was 10 years old. I smashed his head against a tree over and over again. To this day he is deaf in his left ear. I had this bow & arrow set. The arrows had rubber tips on them. There was a girl in the neighborhood that was always bugging me to play with my bow & arrow set. I would yell: *NO! LEAVE ME ALONE!* But she persisted so one day I shot an arrow into her eye. She is blind in that eye now. It was fortunate for her that I did not have a real bow & arrow set because I would have killed her. It would not have upset me in the least. For most of my life, I have been violent. I have gotten into lots of fights, threatened many lives, stolen, cheated, and lied. I didn't care.

I hated people if they weren't part of my dad's inner circle, his *crew*. Ice Pick Sammy, Louie Blue Shoes, et al., were brutal guys with a dark side to them that was downright evil. You would think that such guys, including my dad, would be racist, sexist monsters. But they had a bizarre sensitivity to them. They did not judge people on the color of their skin or their religious backgrounds. Many of my dad's best friends were Jamaican. They were partners in his construction companies. They ran the companies, called the shots. My dad loved his friend Sweet Willie Sweet. He was born in Kingston, Jamaica and had recently moved with his family to the U.S. Willie and his family were always welcome in our home, as we were in his. Willie taught me about West Indian music, Calypso, and Harry Belafonte. My dad and Mom, Willie and his wife, and us kids (we ranged from Willie's youngest, Celestine, who was five, up to me, the oldest, at fifteen) would go see Count Basie at this big amusement park called Freedom Land. I have always been comfortable around people of every ethnicity, color, etc. Of course, you needed to be in the crew for me to really trust you. If I didn't know you, I considered you a potential enemy, not a potential friend. It's difficult to live this way, but it was the only way I knew at that time. If I was in a sad mood and someone looked at me the wrong way it would crush me. I'd think, "Everybody hates me!" I was a little pussy when I was in that mood. But if I were in a bad mood or a macho mood I would not hesitate to pull my knife (I carried a Bowie knife at all times) and threaten your life.

When I was much older, I was assigned a number of hits by my dad. It's not that I didn't try, but none of my designated killings came to fruition. God takes care of idiots like me *and* the guys I was supposed to whack. One time I was told to clip a guy who was infringing on Dad's construction business. So I set up a dinner meeting with the guy, saying that my dad asked me to work out the details for a détente. Dad and the guy had been friends for a hundred years and he knew me from the time I was born. So he trusted me. Big mistake. I was going to pick him up at his house and we were going to drive to his favorite restaurant, which happened to be owned by Dad. The plan from there was that once in the parking lot, I would take my Bowie knife and fillet him. I figured one thrust in his side to disable him and then I'd slit his throat. Simple. I was actually counting the days until the big event. I couldn't wait to break in my knife. It was new. I wanted it to be blood stained. But the guy got the flu. His wife called me that afternoon and said he was puking all night. So somebody else got to kill him a couple months later.

My dad's friend, Ice Pick Sammy, owned a bar called *Sammy's Casino Lounge*. It had red velvet booths and black walls with golden tigers painted on them. We always hung out there. It was the coolest place. I think that's where the seeds of my eventual change of profession to musician were planted. Willie would tell me about the music that the band was playing. He would say the bass player added to the bottom, the drummer was beating out a fat pocket. I was intrigued. I thought: *That's a good job too!* My dad was always singing. Dad encouraged me to study guitar. Eventually I switched to bass.

Anyway, Ice Pick Sammy had a Great Dane named Hercules who lived at the bar. When he stood on his hind legs, Hercules was over six feet tall. He was my best friend. I loved that dog. He lived in the backyard behind the bar, in a big garage. He and I would wrestle, I'd take him for walks and I'd feed him steak. One night after the bar closed, some junkie fuck-head broke into the place and rifled the cash register, which was, of course, empty. No one leaves money in a bar overnight. So the junkie prick goes out back to see if there was anything worth stealing and he runs smack into Hercules barking his head off. The bastard shot Hercules several times in the head and killed him. As soon as Dad found out, around 6AM, he woke me with the news. I cried like a baby and then I became filled with a rage so great that I had never before experienced. I drove to the bar. Hercules was lying on the ground in the garage under a tarp. I didn't look beneath because I wanted to remember my dog the way I had known him, alive, happy, and loving. But I hugged his lifeless form and slipped my hand under the tarp to hold his paw. Death sucks. But at that moment I wanted to bring death to that junkie. I left Hercules for the last time and circled the neighborhood, looking for that scumbag loser or *anyone*, to kill. I was alone, 16 years old, driving without a license and carrying a Bowie knife. At that moment, I was out of my mind. Again, God takes care of idiots because it was early in the morning and no one was up yet. My dad caught up to me and said to come back to the bar. When I got there, Sammy told me the cops had been by to say that they caught the junkie. Dad and Sammy put up the bail money anonymously. As they brought him out, I got a good look at the piece of shit who killed Hercules. I begged my dad to let me butcher the worthless fuck. I wanted to cut him up piece by piece. But Dad said to leave it to Sammy. Within hours of his release, they found the junkie floating in the water under the Throgs

Neck Bridge, down by the docks, his head cut off, his body massacred. Knowing Sammy, it was not a pleasant or a quick death. To this day, I miss my pal Hercules with all my heart.

The Big Game

I've been a bass player since 1965 – that's something like 46 years. Music is the only thing I've ever wanted to do. Except for a minute in 1967 when I thought maybe I'd be an NFL football player. I was big and stupid so why not? I tried out for a local sandlot football team called the Saints – although these guys were anything but. Everyone had colorful names like The Fly, The Flea, Maul, Crusher, Big Boy, Zebby, Crazy Danny… everyone but me. I was Ventura. I hated being called by my last name. Now, I didn't get involved with football because I actually thought I'd make it to the NFL. I mean, that dream pretty much faded the minute it entered my mind. You could get seriously hurt playing football. Besides, I didn't like the number they gave me, "84". I was a center, the jerk-off who hikes the ball, the guy under whose ass another guy sticks his hands every fucking play. If I had to perform in such a manner, I at least wanted the number of my choice, "50". Now that's a good number for a center. But no, I was number "84". I was a football player because I heard that football players get all the girls. Well, that's true to a degree. The quarterback, the fullback, the linebackers, all the glamour boys, they get the girls. The pudgy, not very sexy dumb asses who allow themselves to be beaten to a pulp on the offensive line (like me) get nothing but cuts, bruises, broken noses, broken fingers and, if you're the center like me, some glamour boy quarterback sticking his hands under your ass for you to snap the football to him. Good thing I wore a cup.

So here I am in November 1967, and by some miracle the Saints have beaten the Harlem Chargers, the Archer Street Rams, and the Mt. Vernon Eagles among other very scary and violent teams, to play in the "big game", the championship. I hated football. But after three months of getting my head handed to me on a muddy platter, I figured, "What the fuck, I'll play the big game." We sat in the concrete bunker the home team reserved for the visitors... us. We could feel the walls shake as these mindless hunks of meat punched their lockers, punched each other, and screamed "We're gonna kill those fucking Saints!" Kill a Saint? That's just wrong. So we did the only thing a serious contender for a sandlot football league championship would do in our position… we lit a few fatties laced with angel dust and passed them around the room. It was either that or head for the parking lot because the team next door must have thought we were playing for a zillion dollars or a chance to fuck every pretty girl in the stadium. The guy on the P.A. mic introduces us and we come running out, stoned as crows, feeling invincible and hungry for potato chips. I myself tripped over my friend Charlie and we both fell into a mud puddle. All the pretty girls we were planning on tapping at the beginning of the season were laughing at us. The first play of the game, the opposing kickoff returner ran for a touchdown. I tackled Charlie, who was on my team, because I was so wasted that I didn't know where the fuck I was. When it was our turn, I lined up and the biggest, meanest looking guy I ever saw stood above me. I snapped the ball, and this guy punches me in the mouth, an upper cut to the chin. I bit my mouth guard in half. I felt my vertebrae snap in a chain reaction that made me see flashes of orange for a few minutes. I fell backwards onto our quarterback. In doing so, I broke his finger. He was out. My cousin Gino came in and subbed at quarterback. If you think it's weird having a friend stick his hands under your ass, try having your cousin stick his hands under your ass. *What a fuckin' day.* This went on all afternoon. I'd snap the football, the big linebacker would crush me with a hard-as-steel taped closed fist – either under my chin or on top of my helmet or in the back of my neck. Slowly, though, I was getting his number and began doing some illegal cross body blocking, diving at his feet, causing him to fall over me. It became our own personal war that he won hands down. But I had somehow earned a modicum of his respect because after the last play of the game, he picked me up, patted me on the head and said, "Good game. You're a tough bastard." I said, "Thank you. I hope I never see you again." I limped off the field with my teammates, showered, changed and got on the team bus, a *1949 Piece of Shit*. No one said a word on the ride back home. It took two weeks before I could play my bass again. We had lost *The Big Game*. And I didn't get laid unless you count my cousin sticking his hands under my ass. But, even though I had been used as a punching bag all season long by a succession of muscle-bound giant monsters, I not only survived, I had gained the respect of every one of them. Plus I had proven that even pudgy musicians like me got laid considerably more often than pudgy football players.

Don't Bullshit A Bullshitter

All of the guys in Dad's crew were cool people. They were funny and pretty much always in a good mood. At least that was my experience with them. But they all had tempers and if someone got on their nerves, it could get ugly very quickly. My dad's temper was explosive. He never touched my sister, my mom or me. But anyone else who pissed him off had to watch out. One day we were in Dad's office, the place where he conducted business, but also a place where he partied. The most beautiful women I had ever seen were in and out of the place all the time. Dad could flip-flop between business and pleasure unexpectedly. He hated for people to lie to him but he lied to everyone. He had a saying, "Don't bullshit a bullshitter." It was a real chill afternoon and my dad, some of the guys and girls and I were all watching the baseball game on TV. I was drinking Coca-Cola. The rest of them were drinking rum & Coke. This guy walks in, smiling and happy, and stands in front of my dad, who was sitting on the couch between two super-duper gorgeous women. The guy asks my dad, "Did you take care of that thing you promised?" "Yeah, don't worry about it," my dad answered. "You're a fucking liar…" the guy starts to say but before he could finish the sentence my dad jumped off the couch, clamped his big right hand around the guy's throat and slams his head against the door of the office. The guy was dazed. We were stunned. No one could move. We were frozen. My dad was as quick and agile as a cat but strong as an ox. He smashed this poor bastard's head against the door so hard and so many times that the guy's body went limp, like a rag doll. He not only fractured this jerk-off's skull, he actually popped the door out of the frame. When it was clear that this shithead had seen the error of his ways, Dad let go of the guy and he crumbled into a pile on the floor amidst splinters of wood, plaster, and globs of bloody skull bone. Then Dad went back to the couch and snuggled his ass in between to the two gorgeous babes. "C'mon, Yankees!" he yelled, a big smile on his face. He took a sip of his rum & Coke. If he was the least bit shook by what had just transpired, you could not tell. My dad had ice water in his veins. He was a cool customer. I worshipped him. I still do. I noticed that the guy Dad had just crushed was moaning so I got up to help the fool.

My dad said to me, without taking his eyes off the TV screen, “Leave him there.” As people walked in and out of the office that afternoon and evening, they simply stepped over the dying mobster, who was lying in a giant pool of his own blood, the back of his skull caved in. Around midnight, Dad and I went home. Mom and my sister were asleep. We made a pot of coffee, lounged on the couch for a while, Dad recalling his days as a radioman aboard the SB2C Helldivers in World War II. After an hour or so, he went to his room and I went to mine.

The next morning around 9AM, I awoke to the lovely aroma of bacon and eggs. I walked into the kitchen and Dad was in his chef’s apron, cooking away. Our family sat down to a yummy breakfast and then went to church. It was Sunday.

The Little Shop Of Insanity

As I've probably mentioned, the guys my dad and I used to run with had colorful names: Louie Blue Shoes, Ice Pick Sammy, Fat Patsy, Zoot, Little Vinnie, Big Vinnie, Regular Vinnie, Ace, Smokestack, the list goes on. The girls had good names too: Trans Am Marianne, Marianne Marianne, Sheila Tequila, etc. They all hung out in a club, a little hole in the wall that they called the "Democratic Club" for reasons unknown to me. I know the place was a front for all the illegal stuff they did, plus it was party central. But calling it a democratic club seemed a bit odd, even for them. I called it *The Little Shop of Insanity*. Nonetheless, they treated me well and paid me well. I was comfortable there. One of my jobs was to get the food, because eating was the one ritual around which all other activities revolved. Once, I was asked to pick up an order of Chinese food. The whole crew was there so Patsy told me to buy multiple orders of spare ribs, fried rice, egg rolls, wonton soup, roast pork, you name it. He gave me a wad of $20 bills and sent me on my way. There were too many boxes of food for me to carry back alone so one of the guys from the Chinese restaurant had to help me. When we got back to the club, it was virtually empty. All but a few guys had left. Patsy took out a few containers of spare ribs and said, "bring the rest of it home to your Mom." I went to hand him his change, which had to be $50 (in 1966 money) and he said, "Keep it." At times, I made $200 per week and I was only in high school. It was around this time that I began to give a life of crime serious thought. It was cool because I got to drive their big cars, Cadillacs, Buicks, and Lincolns, even though I didn't have a driver's license. I ran all kinds of errands for them. I once drove 100 miles from the City to the Poconos just to deliver a suit to Patsy, who had forgotten it at the cleaners in our neighborhood. I got $100 for that. In 1966, that was a boatload of money.

One time Patsy got into an argument with Louie over dirt. Patsy had a summer home in the Catskills, as I mentioned, and he said, over lunch of course, that the dirt in the farm region of that upstate New York area was the best in the country. The onions, lettuce and other vegetables produced in this region were more delicious than anywhere else in the United States. Louie said the West Coast has, by far, the best dirt. Patsy actually said to Louie: "You are *UNAMERICAN* if you think that California has better dirt than New York!" Although my dad had many seemingly dim-witted yet extremely crafty, generous, kind, dangerous and scary friends, Fat Patsy was my favorite. He always let me drive his lime green Buick Regal, he taught me about opera, played his Caruso records for me, and introduced me to daVinci and Michelangelo. He was an educated man with a lot of street smarts, but he would say the dumbest stuff. Of course, if you laughed at him you were as good as dead. Patsy gave no thought to bashing a guy's skull to pulp and then sitting down to dinner. Most of those guys were like that. But Patsy was *Il Capo Di Tutti Capi* (the boss of all bosses) and had permission to do so at will. My dad and I were the only ones who could bust his chops without any consequences. He loved my father. They were very close. My dad was 6 feet tall, sleek and muscular and handsome. Patsy was 400 pounds and no Don Juan. But Patsy was very sensitive about his weight and he didn't take kindly to being chided. To do so meant a quick and sure smash in the mouth with Patsy's club-like fist. Patsy was as strong as an ox. But my dad would always say, "Patsy, I love you too much to see you kill yourself. You got to lose some weight." Patsy would shuffle his feet and look down at the floor, "I know, Breezie, and I'm trying." Then Patsy would say he was cutting back from four packs of cigarettes a day to two, that he was joining a gym, etc. It was hilarious to watch. Patsy was like a schoolboy when Dad would get on him about his weight. That was because Patsy and Dad truly loved each other and were as close as brothers.

It was around this time that I began playing in bands and getting very serious about music. Patsy and Dad were huge supporters of my efforts. They would throw block parties just so my band could play. They let us rehearse in the basement of *The Little Shop of Insanity* and they even bought us our first instruments. Dad would drive us to our gigs in a van and stay with us because we were underage. We played in all of Patsy's bars, and he owned a bunch. No one ever bothered us, not even the union or police. It was fun. But I was still torn between a life of crime and a life of music. I was confused. I liked all the cool stuff a life of crime bought: musical instruments, gigs at clubs, driving Cadillacs, eating yummy food in *The Little Shop of Insanity* and always having my pockets bulging with cash.

It's odd that I now hold three collegiate degrees including a Ph.D. I had absolutely no intention of going to college. The only reason I enrolled in university when I was 18 years old was to stay out of the army. The Viet Nam war was raging and I was a prime target to Uncle Sam. Unfortunately, Patsy and my dad had no pull with the military. I was really afraid to go into the Army. I had a feeling I'd never come back. I was not afraid of mob situations because everything was in front of me. I was used to street violence. You could see it happen before the fact. But skulking around in a jungle in Asia at night fighting an unseen enemy was not a very appealing prospect as far as I was concerned. I am really in awe of our military men and women who fight wars overseas so that we can be free. It's somewhat odd to think that the freedom for which they fought at that time included the crime activities of Patsy, Dad and me!

So, I went to college to buy myself four years. I was hoping that the war might be over by the time I graduated. While I was in college, I began to meet some real cool people. Hippies. I enjoyed their company. They were intelligent and civilized and didn't fight. Oddly enough, I did see a guy get killed in college. I was in class when we heard shots. We all ran to the windows just in time to see some guy, I'm guessing a drug dealer because the neighborhood in which my college was located was one of the worst drug neighborhoods in the city, get blown away by the police. He went down hard and his body lay limp on the ground right outside our window. Classes were dismissed for the day and the campus was crawling with detectives. Anyway, I was becoming introduced to a whole new way of life, learning about music like R&B, soul, and artists like James Brown, Buddy Guy and Charles Wright. So I was living a double life of sorts, hippie by day, budding mobster by night. It was actually my dad and Patsy who persuaded me to go full tilt into music. They even let me bring my hippie friends to *The Little Shop of Insanity*. They continued to allow us to rehearse there, to eat there and to hang there. The mobsters and the hippies got along really well. The mob guys saw the hippies as harmless. They enjoyed the music we played, they loved the hippie girls who ran with us and they liked having youth in the club. Most of the guys were old school, at least the guys in *The Little Shop of Insanity*, and they were happy to have the younger kids like us around. It was a beautiful time in my life. I would wander around New York City, check out the music shops, attend classes every now and then, hang out with my girlfriend and chill at *The Little Shop of Insanity*. From 1968 until 1972 life was a total blast. But as graduation drew near, in April 1972, I received my draft notice. Life took a drastic turn. My tranquility was gone. I couldn't sleep. I was a nervous wreck. It seemed Uncle Sam wanted ME!

In the midst of all of this, there was always Fat Patsy with his inimitable quotes:

"She's like a Greek god."

"I love my Buick Regal, it's the Cadillac of Cars."

"I know the guy who drew that painting."

"That fucking guy's tall. He must be 6 foot 12."

"That fucking guy's like a bull in a china shop. What he don't break he shits on."

"Spaghetti is good for you, like spinach for Popeye."

"Needles the junkie is doing much better since rehab. He's a new man. He made a complete 360."

Patsy was a fount of such axioms, but he was also the only guy at the club, other than Dad, with a college degree. My dad graduated from the Chicago Institute of Technology and built a television set in 1943, long before such items were even on the market. Patsy studied Art History and loved classical music. He could tell a Mozart composition from a Haydn, a Renoir painting from a Monet. But he could not master English and was always embarrassed by the Italian/English hybrid slang that he spoke. For example, "Sandwich" was pronounced "Sengwich". Pop and Patsy had a lot in common, including explosive, violent tempers and little patience. Patsy was one of the heads of my dad's crew and had the power to "push a button". This was code. If Patsy "pushed a button", someone died. The circumstances of the execution depended upon Patsy's mood and the offense committed by the unfortunate party. Death could come quickly, a bullet to the back of the head with the guy completely unaware, or slowly, a brutal, merciless routine of torture that included cutting the guy's fingers off one at a time. The goal of this gruesome custom was to get the guy to beg for death. At that point, he would be obliged. Like my dad, Patsy had ice water in his veins. He would listen to the Goldberg Variations, discuss politics with my hippie friends, take care of them, feed them, and clothe them. He loved my hippie friends and they loved him. He would bring sincere joy into the lives of those he loved. He would build shelters for the homeless, give money to the church, buy toys for the neighborhood kids at Christmas and throw block parties in summer. He would send entire groups of underprivileged kids to summer camp. In many ways, he was truly a humanitarian. But he was a ferocious killer with absolutely no regard for human life if that human being broke the unwritten rules by which Patsy and my dad lived. I cannot explain this life. But I can say that it was Patsy, my dad, Sweet Willie, Ice Pick Sammy and all the others in Dad's crew who unintentionally dissuaded me from taking up this life by encouraging me to follow my musical ambitions. Patsy told me to go for a Ph.D. when I didn't even know what that was. My dad, while deep down wishing that I would follow in his footsteps, did encourage me to follow my musical dreams and funded that endeavor when he saw it was what I wanted. Sammy said it's difficult to live with blood on your hands. I don't think it would have been difficult for me. I was born into a world of violence and honed my skills in that little shop of insanity, The Democratic Club.

My dad is in a hospice. Patsy, Sammy, Louie and all the others are dead. I have done as my mentors have instructed. I got an education, including a Ph.D. I built careers in music and in education. But to this day, just behind the mask of civility that I am forced to wear in everyday life, I feel the demons that cursed my dad and Patsy and all the others tempting me. There is no doubt in my mind that the demons of my forefathers could punch through this thin veneer of socially correct behavior at any time and I will reopen the doors of *The Little Shop of Insanity*.

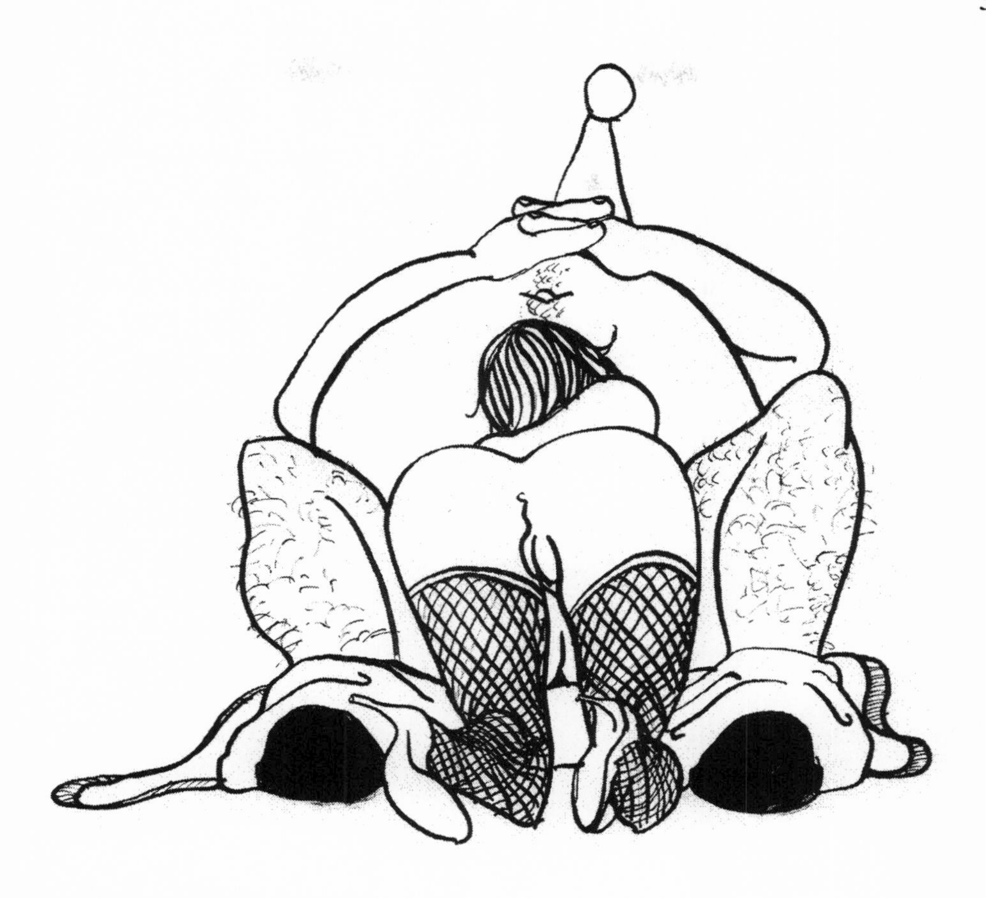

Christmas Insanity

Christmas Eve to New Years Day was a sacred time for the mobsters in the City in the 1960s and 1970s. During that 20-year span, when I was most deeply involved with the business of my dad, Fat Patsy and all the other crazy motherfuckers who ran in that crew, *The Holidays,* as they were called, were a time to celebrate, not to do business. Dad and Fat Patsy threw *two* sets of Christmas parties. One set for the family and one set was for the *"Family"*. Dad made Christmas truly a magical time for my sister, my mom and me. He'd set up his Lionel train sets, decorate the house and entertain all the people who came to visit in the days before Christmas Eve. Dad had a beautiful singing voice and although he sang constantly, all year long, at

Christmas he would sing his favorite song, "The Christmas Song". *Chestnuts roasting on an open fire…* I can hear him right now as clear as ever. I think had he not chosen to be a mobster, he would have tried to make it as a crooner. He sure had the looks and the voice. Dad would hand out $20 bills to every kid he saw; he tipped everybody. He especially tipped waitresses; 100% of the bill. You just knew when he was going to be returning to the restaurant after he dropped Mom, my sister and me back home. The bill would be $50 and he'd hand the waitress $100, saying keep the change. There would be a look in her eye and I'd say to myself, *"Looks like Pop's tapping this tonight!"* Like Fredo, that guy banged cocktail waitresses two at a time. The Christmas parties went on every night.

While the *capos* still kept a close eye on things, business was put on the back burner until after the New Year. In those days, the mob guys had long memories. I remember at a Christmas party one year, some buffoon got drunk and told Patsy that he was involved in a heist within Patsy's territory. One of the things Patsy and the crew did was hijack trucks and sell the goods. Someone had been pirating the pirated trucks and my dad and Patsy could never figure out who it was. So this drunken jerk-off says, "I really had you guys going! I'd be shooting pool in the club every night watching you guys drive yourselves crazy trying to figure out who did the deed."

Patsy says, "No shit, *cump (another Italian slang for 'friend')*, that was you? You are good, my friend."

"No hard feelings?" the stupid fuck asked.

"Of course not," said Patsy, "you beat us to the punch, fair and square."

They shook hands and I said to myself, *Dead Man Walking*. The cops found the idiot on January 2nd in an abandoned building in Brooklyn. His face had been blown off, compliments of a 12 gauge shotgun. His hands had been chopped off as well. According to the coroner's report, this had been done prior to the fatal shotgun blast.

The Christmas party at *The Little Shop of Insanity* was the best of all. That was for the FAMILY, *La Familia*. No personal families allowed. When I was older and playing in bands, my dad would have us play. It was lunacy. Everyone danced and laughed and ate and drank (except me, I always preferred Coca-Cola, and then Diet Coca-Cola).There were at least a dozen call girls at every one of these parties. Dad would always get me a call girl just for myself. *I loved Christmas*. Every time guys threw parties, my band played at them and we all got call girls. What a wonderful time in my life. I was sixteen, seventeen, eighteen, playing gigs, getting paid and getting blowjobs from gorgeous women. Most of the guys in the crew owned nightclubs. I've been playing my bass before live audiences for a good portion of my life. Up until I was married to my second wife, Patty, the call girls were just part of our pay. The parties held at the *Little Shop of Insanity* were catered, and there was just a ridiculous amount of food, far more than we could have consumed. I found the number of wanted criminals sitting at the dinner table to be amazing. There was an FBI van across the street at all times. Patsy would send out trays of food and Coca-Colas to the Feds. He said it was the least he could do since they had to work on Christmas because of him. The Feds ate like kings and after a while they were all volunteering for stakeout duty. Of course, there were no windows in the club and the door was steel core. We swept the place for bugs and other surveillance devices everyday. The Feds watched us most closely during the holidays. There was no tension at all at this time of year since every one of these monsters was an intimate of Dad and Patsy. New Years Eve was absolutely wild. They would throw at huge bash in *The Little Shop of Insanity* and of course my band would play. We would have all the wives and kids there so we couldn't have the call girls. I really hated to see Christmas season end. It was a glorious time.

As I grew older things changed a bit. While I was living at home, my dad really made Christmas a special season. It was fun, 24/7. But when I got married to my first wife, things changed. I'd have to be considerate and spend Christmas at her family's house. Her Dad was an FBI agent and my father steadfastly avoided him. Although Dad got along with my first wife well, nobody else did. It put a terrible strain on my relationships with my mom and my sister. It was the weirdest thing but when my first wife and I finally divorced, my family celebrated. She was just as happy to be rid of me.

I was a total dick back then. I don't blame her for leaving.

Dad was fond of her, as I said. He maintained a friendship with her that lasted for years. I didn't care.

I was still working for Dad and his crew but in my heart I really wanted to pursue a career as a professional musician. My father even got up and sang with my band a few times. I'll never forget the time that we were playing a local mob dance at the church hall (all these killer gangsters went to church every Sunday). I was playing with a group called *The Sounds Incorporated.* Shitty name, I know. It was 1976. Dad got up and sang *The Theme From The Godfather (Speak Softly Love).* What else? When he finished, the crowd went nuts, cheering. My dad leaned over and kissed me on the cheek. He had a tear in his eye. I know he was always rooting for me to succeed in music. After years of struggle, I finally achieved my dream (and Dad's), having produced and played bass on a number of hit albums and singles.

But time marches on. Things change. I can recall with vivid clarity so many happy times and sad times throughout the years. I know I cannot go back to yesterday. I only have now because no one knows what tomorrow holds. But even now, I smile when I think that my dad bought me women for Christmas. I'm pretty sure Dad even got Santa laid. Christmas is not so happy a time as it once was. It is still a magical time, with lights everywhere and smiling faces and "Merry Christmas!" on everyone's lips. But I see my dad suffering in his private hell, consumed by Alzheimer's, and it makes me so sad. I think, though, if my Pop was able to speak now he'd say:

Essere Felice! (Be Happy!)

He was never one to be bothered by much. He was a natural at making people happy, as proven by those wonderfully insane Christmases that he and Patsy threw. I can still hear Dad singing and greeting everyone who crossed the threshold of *The Little Shop of Insanity*:

BUON NATALE! (MERRY CHRISTMAS!)

I Know Where The Bodies Are Buried

I never got to kill anyone, much to my dismay. It was always something I wanted to do. It's on my bucket list now. The closest I ever got to murder was cleaning up the mess afterwards. My job was to dispose of the bodies. My dad, Fat Patsy and their crew didn't take the guy out to a faraway swamp to kill him. They shot the motherfucker where he stood. Very often, it was in *The Little Shop of Insanity.* One of the crew would hammer some jerk-off and his brains would be splattered all over the floor and the walls. Then the guys would go about their business and Dad would say, *"Trouble, clean this mess up."* That would mean, in addition to scrubbing the place down for the umpteenth time, I'd have to get rid of the body. This was a rather daunting task in so much as there are only so many places one can stash a corpse. The dead guy himself didn't bother me at all. To me, he was a sack of shit in life so in death he was just a dead sack of shit. I never got angry with my dad or any of the guys for not allowing me to hit one of these fuck-heads. But I found it frustrating. I had an inner desire to kill people, like Billy the Kid used to do. *Bang, Bang, Bang.* However, it was not to be. Patsy and Dad were trying to shield me, I suppose, from the gangster life, at least until I was older. So for the moment I had to be content to be a *Mobster-In-Training.*

I would clean the blood and brains up with run-of-the-mill cleaning agents. That was the easy part. It took time but it was easy. Meantime, a couple of the guys would carry the stiff out into the back yard. We had a pergola with grape vines, wisteria, honeysuckle, and other such shrubs growing all over it. It hid the goings-on in the yard quite nicely. We had high wooden fences all around the perimeter of the yard too. There was no way to see in. Plus, the neighbors knew the consequences of snooping. I'd leave the corpse out there for days in the dead of winter. It froze solid within a day or so. Once frozen, I just fired up the chainsaw and cut the fucking thing up into little pieces. Then I'd put pieces into a few garbage bags and haul the bags to the dump. That would be the end of that. The problem was a bit more complicated in the warm weather. I much preferred that Patsy waited until winter to whack people but he was not considerate in that respect. In the warm weather, I had to act quickly as far as disposing of the bodies. It got to be a pain in the ass. I would put the stiff in the trunk of Patsy's big Buick and drive out to Staten Island. As I have mentioned, all the guys had these magic police tags hanging from the rear view mirror. No one ever bothered me even though I was 16 and driving without a license. My dad, Fat Patsy, and all the *Dons* were so fucking connected. They even partnered with the cops. It was amazing. On Staten Island, I would dump the dead guy down a sewer. If he were small enough, in the middle of nowhere. We didn't care if the motherfucker was eventually found. Those corpses decomposed quickly. By the time it got jammed in a pipeline it was beyond recognition. Besides, the police and the D.A. didn't give a rat's ass about another dead mobster. It was just a hassle for me to bring the damned thing to some out of the way, Godforsaken place and dump it. It was even more of a hassle if the guy was a big boy. Then it might take three or four of us to lift the fat fuck and throw him in the trunk of the car. It was also very difficult to stuff a jumbo dead dude through a manhole cover. So we'd have to be creative. We'd usually find a deserted stretch of road, bring the van and push the fat pig out the back onto the pavement. Then we'd run the truck over him, back and forth, until we flattened the son of a bitch. We'd mash him up beyond detection. We'd squash the guy into a pancake, and we'd make sure his head was *gone.* No dental records. Basically, when we were done, you couldn't tell if it was a dog or a man or a deer. Then we'd shovel the pieces into a swamp or bay or whatever was nearby. One time we shoveled the squished mobster into garbage bags and left them in someone's garbage cans. The cans were out on the street so it was garbage day next morning. We never heard a word about it so we have to thank the New York City Department of Sanitation for helping us with that one. Still, this was becoming too much work. I had Fat Patsy buy a big freezer. It was a deluxe model, big enough to hold even the fattest pig. Every time a guy was whacked in *The Little Shop of Insanity* or someplace where we could not simply abandon the corpse, we would drop his ass in the freezer until he was as solid as a rock. Then I would get out my chainsaw and dice the motherfucker. One quick trip to the dump and another job was done and done well.

Unfortunately, I didn't get to pull the trigger but I felt useful in the execution nonetheless. I had little regard for humans, other than our crew, when they were alive. I held absolutely no regard for dead motherfuckers. To me, they were pig food. I don't regret any of the stuff I did back then. I felt most alive when I was witnessing people getting killed. It always astonished me how clueless these stupid fucks were. They would walk into *The Little Shop of Insanity* expecting always to be greeted with open arms. Instead, they served themselves up to the executioner. Never once did they suspect a thing. I loved to see that *last* expression on the face of a guy about to get shot through the head. It was a combination of *What The Fuck?* Then, *Oh Fuck!* And finally, *Get It Over With.* It was really cool. I enjoyed watching the motherfucker take his last breath. Then as his body became still, sometimes the guys would say a prayer for his soul. I mean it. They would pray for The Lord to accept the guy's soul into Heaven.

I'd say to Patsy, "*You just shot the fuck. Why are you praying for his soul?*" Patsy would say, "*He broke the rules and he had to pay. He took an oath and he broke that oath.*" Patsy would sigh, as if weighted by what he had just done. He would continue, *"To us, your people, this is a serious thing. We honor that oath. We did what we had to do, what our fathers and grandfathers did. But all 'morti' (the dead) deserve to be accepted by God into Eternal Rest."*

I would let it go but to me it was bullshit. When the guy would stop breathing I would turn up the freezer and oil the chainsaw. It was just another day at the office. I saw it as simple, honest work.

I know where all the bodies are buried. I buried them.

It Wasn't All Murder

As I have written in other parts of this book, the guys in the crew were not terribly skilled as to proper usages of the English language, or as they called it, *American:*

"*That fucking grease ball is right off the boat, he don't speak American.*"

Of course, neither did any of the crew. They used the word "ain't" far too often. Worse, they coupled it with "got." They also mixed their metaphors.

"That motherfucker ain't got a snowball's chance in heaven."

The curse words and other colloquialisms were often in Italian:

Vaffanculo (Fuck You)

Merda (Shit)

Puttana (Whore)

Sacco di Merda (Scumbag)

Dio Damn It (God Damn It)

Dio Mio (My God)

Buffone (Buffoon)

Figlio Di Puttana (Motherfucker)

Cazzo (Prick)

Culo (Ass)

Bastardo (Bastard)

Cagna (Bitch)

Va Fa Napoli (Go To Hell)

Oobatz (Crazy)

Vig (Interest on a loan from a mobster)

The list goes on and on.

Another unique feature of the mob colloquialisms include the hybrid curse words. My dad was amazing at stringing together multisyllabic curse words:

"*You no-good-mother-God-damned-fucking-rat-fucking-bastard-piece-of-shit-from-the-pussy-of-a-puttana-cagna-bitch-motherless-fucking-scumbag.*"

Notice that he pronounced the damnation bilingually.

Of course, one cannot omit the one-of-a-kind phrases that spewed forth from the mouths of these charming monsters.

Ain't that a nice painting? I know the guy that drew that.

That's just a figment of speech.

You gotta do what you gotta do, what could you do?

You was the one who was out til 9 o'clock in the afternoon!

Nicky? Nicky who?

Charlie? Charlie who?

Eksettera (et cetera)

Can I cop a plea?

Aiight (alright)

What are you, a fucking comedian?

See that broad? I fucked her.

I'll have the fettuccini alla carbonara.

I'm not sayin', I'm just sayin'.

Fuck that motherfucker.

Go fuck your mother in hell.

I think Patsy & Ralphie win the "Most Hilarious Dialogue By Two Gangsters" Award with this little exchange:

Patsy: *Did you do that thing for me?*

Ralphie: *Which thing? The first thing or the second thing?*

Patsy: *The first thing!*

Ralphie: *No, I did the second thing.*

Patsy: *Why did you do the second thing first?*

Ralphie: *Well, I figured I'd do the second thing first and the first thing second.*

Patsy: *Oh. Good call.*

The Little Shop of Insanity was party central. None of the wives were particularly happy that their husbands spent so much time there. Sometimes it was actually difficult for them to get out of the house. Their wives would really put up a fuss. These weren't petite little women. Their wives were *beautiful* but tougher and crazier than the mob guys. They were every bit as violent and far scarier when they were pissed off. (That also made them very sexy!) One day I was with Fat Patsy at his house and I witnessed this little dialogue:

Patsy's Wife: *"Patsy, we're going out to the movies tonight, right?"*

Patsy: *"I can't."*

Patsy's Wife: *"Why not?"*

Patsy: *"I gotta go out."*

Patsy's Wife: *"Where are you going?"*

Patsy: *"You know where!"*

Patsy's Wife: *"I DON'T WANT YOU GOING THERE!"*

Patsy: "*Where?"*

As I began to get into my college experience and meet folks who came from somewhat more diverse backgrounds than I did, I became aware of distinct differences between my family and those of others. Most, if not all, of my friends have not blown up cars, witnessed savage murders, or made thousands of dollars picking up Chinese food for mobsters. None of them received a call girl for their 16th birthday. I still had nothing but love and respect for Dad and his gang of maniacs. I simply began to realize that culture was a nice thing. I enjoyed going to museums, to the opera, and to the theater. I still had no problem ripping someone's gut open with my Bowie knife, which came everywhere with me. I took pleasure in doing other things too. I had a girlfriend named Sunflower Rainbow Sky, or Sky for short. She was part Italian and part Native American. She had long, black flowing hair, and a slim, trim figure with the most delectable titties. Every inch of her was mouth-watering. Plus she was so smart that it was sexy. The guys at *The Little Shop of Insanity* loved her. At Christmas time, they showered her with lots of expensive gifts. They knew she was a hippie and smoked a lot of weed, so they bought her bongs, pipes, leather bags, and all kinds of paraphernalia. Plus they gave her tons of cash. She was very comfortable in this den of iniquity. She was at home among the motley crew of murderers and thieves. It was a great time in my life. The club would be empty and quiet and I'd be fucking Sky in the back room. Out of nowhere, I'd hear, *ATTA BOY, TROUBLE! TAP IT, BABY. TAP IT!* They'd all laugh like a bunch of naughty schoolboys. I'd yell out to them, *ASSHOLES!!!* Sky didn't care. She'd walk to the door, topless, and say, "*Now, boys, behave yourselves.*" All you'd hear was, *WHOOOOOOOOOOO!!!!!! MADONNA!*

It was a shame those days had to end. For all their improper use of language, the way they absolutely butchered the Italian language and the English (or "American") language, I felt a strange sense of warmth, honor and love among these crazy *bastardos.* I knew that I was utterly insulated and protected from everyone and everything. I knew that I would never want for anything and I *thought* the party would never end. It almost didn't. It went on for a long time. It still goes on and on in my mind. But all these guys are dead now. My dad and Zoot are the last of the lot. Their minds and bodies are shot.

I haven't seen Sky in 35 years. She could be a *Grandma* now. If so, I'd *LOVE* to meet her grandchildren. I'd say to them:

"Hey, kids, guess what? Granny used to flash her tits at mob guys for a laugh!"

The party rages on in my mind.

Benny Radar

There was a guy in my dad's crew who was deaf. We called him "Benny Radar". He could feel vibrations in the air, on the ground and on objects. You could not sneak up on him. Impossible. He had the most bizarre manner of speech. Because he had no hearing, his pronunciation was somewhat garbled. For instance, if he wanted to say, "two feet," he pronounced it, "*ooo eeet.*" If he wanted to say, "fuck that scumbag," he pronounced it, "*uck at umbag.*" It got a bit complicated when he would have a conversation with you. But the guys picked up on his lingo years ago and it was the funniest thing to hear them converse, even when they were planning a hit. I would be rolling on the floor as I witnessed this strange tête-à-tête:

Fat Patsy: *Benny, did you pick up that bag of money from that motherfucker?*

Benny Radar: *Oh! Ee ed ee idnt ab oh ash ut ees ood or it. (No! He said he had no cash but he's good for it.)*

Fat Patsy: *Benny, I had enough of this guy's bullshit. Go there with a baseball bat and break his leg.*

Benny Radar: *Ah ee, oo old im ee oud ab oo or eeks. I e embor. (Patsy, you told him he could have two more weeks. I remember.)*

Fat Patsy: *Well, I changed my mind. Go take care of this thing now.*

Benny Radar: *Aw iiit Ah ee. Ah ing I ooo eee ill ugga. (Alright Patsy. I'll bring my Louisville Slugger.)*

These two screwballs are planning to break a guy's legs with a baseball bat and I'm *dying laughing* listening to this. If you didn't know Benny's language - I called it *Benglish* - there is no way you could understand a word he said. But we all understood him. Truly, it was like a comedy routine, but these guys were killers. Benny Radar was bald, with a horseshoe of hair around the bottom of his head. He had a bit of a paunch, stood no more than five feet three inches tall, was deaf, about 70 years old, and he was one of the most ruthless murderers I have ever known. I've watched him beat guys into a pile of red meat and bone chips by himself. He was amazing. When he was swinging that bat, he didn't stop until he completed his mission, whatever "thing" he was assigned. If he was to break someone's leg, that's what he did. One swing, neat and lightning quick, would put the most fearsome brute on the ground, screaming in pain. That was scary to see. Then it would become a comedy routine as Benny would warn the guy not to fuck up again:

Benny: *I et-ing oo et aw e e is im. Ex im ah een inis. (I'm letting you off easy this time. Next time, I'll mean business.)*

The poor bastard would be in a world of pain with a broken leg, looking up from the floor at this 70-year-old bald & deaf maniac, mumbling, *What the fuck did he just say?*

I would break his balls endlessly. Since Benny could read my lips I would speak to him in his language, *Benglish*. This pissed him off so much, but it was so much fun. I'd say to him:

N E, Ut ooo ooo ahn or unch? (Benny, what do you want for lunch?)

Benny was get furious with me:

O e ah mak ooo. Ooooona ahn I. (Trouble, I'll smack you! Tuna on rye.) Then he'd smile at me and swing an air bat as if he were swinging a real bat. I would *not* want to be crushed by one of Benny's swing-for-the-fences cuts.

Everybody loved Benny. Well, everyone except the guys he mauled with his Louisville Slugger. We found him in The *Little Shop of Insanity* one afternoon lying on the couch as usual, eyes closed. Everything looked normal. He had lain down to take a nap. I walked over to him to bust his chops:

N E ache ut. (Benny, wake up.)

But he didn't stir. I gently shook him:

Benny boy, get up. I'll treat you to a tuna on rye. But he didn't move.

I called Patsy. He felt for a pulse but there was none. Benny had a heart attack in his sleep. At his funeral, he looked like he could get up and swing that bat of his. I wanted him to. I felt like shit because I made fun of his speech, not knowing he had just died. Patsy told me later that Benny was still warm when he touched him. He must have died minutes before we got there. I never forgave myself for disrespecting him when he was alive. I know Benny didn't take it to heart. He was a grown man and I was a stupid fucking kid. But I prayed to Benny many and many a night, *Please forgive me for breaking your balls, Benny. I love you.*

In my heart, I know he heard me and forgave me. Now if I could only forgive myself.

Zoot

My dad had a lot of friends, many of them lifelong, and the best of the best was Zoot. Dad and Zoot were hardcore. They drank hard, partied hard, womanized hard and worked hard. This latter verb "worked" meant, in this case, "to kill, to steal, and to make book". If you fucked with Dad and Zoot then the wrath of hell chased you like a swarm of pissed off killer bees. You were fucked.

Dad and Zoot owned racehorses. They'd travel to racetracks all over the country and I'd get to go with them. They were as deeply involved with that very serious sect of the underworld as they were with loan sharks, gambling, and hits. Those two were trouble. Together, they were two invisible stealth fighter jets homing in on a target. You never knew what hit you. Before you could say "Huh?" you were gone, dead, *morto*. They incinerated people. They took great care and pride in planning their hits. When they hit you, there was nothing left except teeth. They loved their work. Dad only hit people in partnership with Zoot. It was always a two-man operation. I was with them on most "jobs". When the other fathers in our neighborhood brought their kids to work, it was to some stuffy office to watch Dad push a pencil all day. When my dad brought me to work, it was to watch him kill a guy. *That was fun!* There was nothing boring about my dad's work. I used to laugh as I witnessed some chump beg for his life:

Soon-To-Be-Dead-Guy: *Breezie, please! This is all a misunderstanding!*

Dad: *Really? Jimmy Bugs saw you fucking with my horse's leg. Then, what do you know, he goes lame in the next race! Was that a coincidence?*

Soon-To-Be-Dead-Guy: *That wasn't me! Jimmy Bugs is mistaken! I love you and Zoot, Breezie. I'd never do anything like that. Right, Zoot? Tell him!*

Zoot: *I think you're a lying son of a bitch so don't ask me.*

Soon-To-Be-Dead-Guy: *Guys! Please!*

Dad: *Just tell the truth. If you do, we'll go easy on you. Did you fuck with my horse's leg?*

Soon-To-Be-Dead-Guy: *OK! Yes! I'm sorry, guys. I know it was wrong. Please, cut me a break!*

Dad: *See? Wasn't that easy? Don't you feel better?*

Soon-To-Be-Dead-Guy: *Yes, Breezie. So you're going to go easy on me?*

Dad: *Yes, of course!*

Soon-To-Be-Dead-Guy: *Thank God!!!*

Dad: *Why are you thanking God? You're still going to die. But we'll make it quick...*

Before the Soon-To-Be-Dead-Guy could say another word, Zoot put a slug right between his lying eyes. I used to get the biggest kick from seeing shit like this. Stupid fuck.

We had to meet a guy at Dad & Zoot's office, a construction company, to *"take care of a thing."* The guy thought he was going to discuss possibly doing some renovation work in one of Dad's restaurants. They set the meeting at night after everyone went home. Dad and Zoot knew this guy for years and he trusted them. *Stolto. (Fool.)* We walked in to the office with bottles of wine, liquor, Coca-Cola for me of course, and we actually sat around and chatted for almost an hour. Dad and Zoot seemed genuinely interested in knowing how his family was, how business was, did he think the Yankees were going to win the Pennant? Zoot said, "You know, we love you. That's why we're giving you this big renovation job." The guy said, "I love you guys too." But somewhere along the line he had fucked Dad and Zoot. I don't know how. I don't know the details. I'm sure the guy didn't even know he screwed up. He probably thought whatever he did was within that unwritten but strictly enforced set of rules by which Dad, Zoot, Fat Patsy and all the rest of these mobsters lived. The guy seemed to me to be clueless.

I was thinking about saying to my dad, "Pop, shouldn't we get going?" That was code. That meant that something was wrong. Wait. At that point, my dad would have looked me straight in the eye. We would have had a silent conversation. It was actually eerie for people to see us do this. All I'm saying is that the guy probably didn't even break the unwritten rules. At least that was my instinct. My dad could read my mind. In the blink of an eye, he would determine if my hesitation was founded or not. Dad might have hesitated, spoken to the guy more and possibly delayed the hit. Dad and Zoot spoke to each other in this manner all the time. They would go into a trance, looking into each other's eyes, communicating silently. It was frightening and fascinating at the same time. Anyway, I decided not to say anything to Dad. What the fuck did I care if this jerk-off lived or died? It didn't mean shit to me. So, I kept my mouth shut and the hit went on as planned. Amidst the laughter and drinking and discussions of renovations, my dad, seemingly out of thin air, throws a glassful of pure alcohol into the guy's face. Before the guy could even scream, I mean before he took his next breath, Zoot hit him right in the eyes with a stream of flame from a can of butane. I don't even know where he had it hidden. All I know is the guy's head burst into flames. Snap your fingers. That's how fast it happened. Then my dad grabbed a bottle of gasoline that had been stashed in with the liquor, beer and Coca-Cola bottles, and smashed it at the guy's feet. Zoot gave it a shot from the can of butane and the guy went up like a dried out Christmas tree. He actually exploded. Pop, Zoot and I watched for a second or two. It was awesome. I was amazed. *How cool my dad is!* Dad and Zoot wanted to see if the physics of their dark plan worked to their satisfaction. Then we simply walked out of the building and across the street to a diner. As the fire engines and cop cars raced by, we sat in a booth, drank coffee, ate scrambled eggs and watched them try to put out the fire. The entire building became a torch.

Dad: *"Zoot, next time we need to use a different accelerant. I'm not happy with the ratio of air to starter. Maybe we'll try a petroleum distillate."*

Zoot: *"I think you're right. I was really hoping we collapsed the building but I can see it's going to stand after all. We need to generate more heat."*

Trouble (Me*): "Yummy eggs!"*

At this point in my young life, killing was fun and games. I didn't care. I was safe. My dad was invincible. Fat Patsy, Zoot, Ice Pick Sammy and every one of the guys would never allow anything to happen to me. I had already done some extremely violent things, but I didn't give a rat's ass. No one could touch me. No one would even try. My dad and Zoot had just made a guy explode. There was not a soul on earth who could get near me.

My friends, the children of Zoot, Fat Patsy, Sweet Willie, et al. and I were terrors. On the one hand, we were quiet, shy, respectful. On the other, we'd steal anything that wasn't nailed down and if given the word by Fat Patsy or Dad, we would descend upon an unsuspecting guy like a squadron of demonic birds of prey. We would beat him, bite him, claw him and kick him to within an inch of his life. We were only used as a warning. The guy well knew that the next visit would not be from us and would not be as pleasurable. I look back upon those days now and I am utterly amazed by the physical damage my friends and I, little fiends that we were, inflicted on people. Equally amazing to me is that I still don't care. I have no remorse regarding the people we crippled or maimed. My dad taught me well.

Although I have built a life for myself and have been blessed far beyond my meager worth, there is still something growing within me. I don't even see it as evil. I simply see it as who I am. My doctors control my temper with drugs, my trainer controls my aggression with fitness workouts, and my cardiologist controls my blood pressure with medications. But I still hear Zoot's voice saying, "You are who you are. Never forget that." Zoot is an invalid now. His reign of terror is over. My dad suffers from Alzheimer's now and that big, strong, strapping man has finally wilted. But Dad still has the power to speak to me with his mind, even when he's at his worst, when it is obvious that the disease is winning the war. He still looks right into my eyes and I can understand him. Sometimes he says to me, "Get me out of this broken body." Sometimes he says to me, "I wish I could play Briscola with you again." The last words my dad actually spoke to me were, "Is this it?" and right after that, "I love you." Since then he's been speaking to me without words, just with his eyes. Dad and Zoot still talk to each other with their eyes as well. They sit across the room from one another and look off into space. Then, without the slightest sign that it's coming, they will turn, at the same time, and look right into each other's eyes. When I see this, a chill runs down my spine. I know they are speaking to each other, discussing a hit they did 50 years ago, and saying: *Nobody fucked with us!*

Smokey

I called the guys in my dad's crew "Uncle" even though they were not blood relations. They all treated me like family nonetheless. But I did have one or two real uncles who were also members of the crew. One such character, and I write this with a heart full of love, was my Uncle Smokey. Smokey puffed a big cigar all the time. Dad gave him the name "*Smokestack*" many years ago. It was shortened to Smokey over time. I was as stupid as they came when I was a kid of 20 or so. I pretty much stayed stupid until I was about 50 years old, but that's beside the point. I never meant any disrespect but I would call him "Old Man" a lot (far too much). He was 50 years old when I was 20 years old. But Uncle Smokey was an ex-boxer, at 50 still lightning fast with his fists. You did not want Uncle Smokey on your trail. He was afraid of *nothing*. If someone was dumb enough to piss off Uncle Smokey by honking for him to move at a traffic light, for instance, things could get ugly really quick. When such an incident happened, I've seen him get out of his car and walk back to the driver that honked at him. If the driver was anyone but a woman or senior citizen, Smokey would practically rip the car door open and tell the guy to get out. If the guy wouldn't oblige, Smokey would pull the guy out of the car through the window. That was so cool to watch. The guy would crap his pants. "Got a problem, Buddy?" Smokey would ask. "No problem," was always the reply.

One day I was busting Smokey's chops, calling him "old". I said that I could beat him in a boxing match. That was playing with dynamite, although most of the time Uncle Smokey would just laugh and say something like, "Dream on." On this day, Uncle Smokey decided to "warn" me. No sooner had the words "Old Man" come out of my mouth than a muscular arm propelled a rock-like fist directly at my nose. Had Uncle Smokey hit me he would have knocked me into next week. But his fist stopped an inch away from my face. I didn't even have time to move. He smiled and said, "I have one or two rounds left in me, anytime you feel like jumping into the ring." That was the last time I ever called Uncle Smokey "old". Smokey was a southpaw. While you had your eye on his right fist, his left came up from the floor like a torpedo. You never saw it. It was just lights out. One time I was sparring with him, just getting some exercise. He always had me wear a helmet with a face guard so I wouldn't get hurt if he slipped. We really hit each other, though not hard. But Smokey did slip once. I swear to you I was closing in slowly, getting ready to throw a round house at him. That's all I remember. I awoke to beer splashing on my face as Uncle Smokey poured the contents of his Budweiser on me. He helped me up, dusted me off and said, "Ready?" I said, "No way, Uncle Smokey, I'm done for today." I have no idea where that punch came from. All I know is my jaw was swollen for two days and hurt like hell for two weeks. Years later, at Uncle Smokey's funeral, I stood at his open coffin and looked upon that tough-guy face I had come to love and respect. "*You could probably STILL kick my ass, Uncle Smokey.*"

Today kids call me "Old Man". I know that to be young is to be stupid. So I let it go. But there are times that I am tempted to show them the full measure of my viciousness and my total disregard for life. There are times I could kill them with no second thought. I loved violence. I loved that life. It was stressful but it was fun at the same time. Our mantra was, *fuck everybody.* We did what we wanted. *Fuck you.* I have to pray constantly to maintain my composure with young punks who call me "Old Man" like I did to Smokey. My Uncle Smokey loved me so he would never hurt me. He taught me to fight, to box. He nurtured me. We had so much fun together. But I don't love the punks who think they're cool. I have come close to destroying three of them. I lost it, but instead of attacking them, I threw whatever object was nearest to me against the wall. This was always enough to chill the little limp dick fuckheads. I pray a lot. I need the Lord's help to keep cool. I want so badly to lose it again. There is so much venom within me. Young people are so dim. I know they have inflated senses of self. It's not their fault. That's how young people are wired. But I'm tired of their shit. I'm tired of being called "Old Man" in the media and by these unfeeling little scumbag kids. There is a bit of Smokey in me. There is a bit of all the guys in the crew in me. Smokey, Dad and all the rest were fierce characters and they are all alive in me. The brutality, ferocity and rage, those undeniable demons that lived just below the surface of their charming demeanors, live on in me.

Giovani I pisciari su di voi. (Young punks, I piss on you.)

The Art Class

It was no secret that the only reason I went for my undergraduate degree was to stay out of the Viet Nam War. It was 1968 and I had no desire to die in the jungles of some faraway place, much as I revered those who did. It was just that the Army did not suit my lifestyle. You had to get up early, something that mobsters and musicians did not do. So whatever path I chose, waking at sunup was not in the cards. I did enjoy riding the subway to school, a college in Brooklyn, USA. However, I spent most of my time running around Manhattan. Times Square was my favorite haunt. There were excellent Italian restaurants and block after block of music stores. I much preferred Times Square to school. The major I chose was *marketing.* I didn't even know what the fuck marketing was. I told the guidance counselor in high school that I wanted to be a musician. I didn't think he'd look upon me with fondness if my proposed career choice were *mobster.* The guidance counselor was a total dick. He was a pompous, holier-than-thou scumbag who looked down his nose at the students, as if this shithead was doing something special for the world. Mr. Douchebag said that there was no money in music and that I should choose *advertising* as my career. I said to him, in earnest, *"The Beatles are doing OK."* He reached across the desk and smacked me across the face. At that point it was only a matter of time before the self-righteous fuck died. Anyway, I didn't give a shit what my college major was as long as it kept me out of the Army.

As an aside, I went home that night and told my dad that the guidance counselor slapped me. The next morning, an elite army of hit men waited in a van in the parking lot of the high school. The words *Facility Maintenance* were printed across each side of the van. When the guidance counselor stepped out of his car, the van swung around and the guys pulled him inside. It was quick, neat and quiet. That was the end of the guidance counselor. He was never seen again. My only regret is that Dad said I had to go to classes that day. I was not allowed to miss school over a scumbag like the guidance counselor. Another opportunity to kill a fuck-head and again I am denied! Anyway, the piece of shit died a brutal death, I am sure.

After all that, I did choose *marketing* as my major in college. Like I said, I didn't care. College was fun, except for the classes. I really did not enjoy sitting in a classroom listening to some boring fart-faced professor going on and on about economics and selling the sizzle not the steak. What a snore fest. The girls were cute and I dated a lot of them. I brought them to *The Little Shop of Insanity* and introduced them to the guys. The hippie girls loved it there. They were very comfortable among these ruthless killers. Go figure. I never told the girls that my dad, Patsy and the rest were mobsters. But they thought it was cute that I hung around with my father. They didn't know the half of it. I ran around with the hippie girls, hung out in Times Square, rode the subways and did a lot of other fun things. The one thing I did not do was go to class. I ended up on academic probation and that woke me up. So I tried to enroll in courses that I might enjoy. Among my good friends in college was a total burnout whose name was Space Ranger Gary. He was high every waking hour. He dropped a ton of acid, thus the *Space Ranger* moniker. He mentioned to me that there was an art class he had taken the semester before and that *naked female models* posed for the students. *WHAT?* Gary told me that the girls were beautiful and stark naked. They posed in every sort of position. Nothing was left to the imagination. *Fucking A. Count me in.* I enrolled in the course and when the first day of class rolled around, I was front and center. I had a boner just waiting for class to start. Soon the professor came in and lectured us on classroom etiquette and deportment:

This is not a chance to ogle the models. (Yeah, right.)

You may not make lewd comments. (Can I ask her to bend over?)

You may not take photos. (How can I practice at home?)

These are professional models. (Does that mean they give blowjobs too?)

His boring introduction almost made me lose my boner. *Come on, Professor Whoever, get the fucking broad out here!* He calls her and from a side door walks a *behemoth* of a woman. She was 300 pounds, easily. She had a forest growing from each armpit. The hair on her pussy went down her thighs like Elvis' sideburns. Her legs were hairy down to her ankles. She had rolls of fat cascading down her chin, her belly, her hips and her ass. Her tits were giant water balloons that hung straight down. If I was stranded alone on a desert island and she was the only woman, I would rather fuck a monkey. *How the fuck was I supposed to draw this fucking elephant? I couldn't even look at her.* To top it off, she was posing in ways that were revolting. Was it necessary for her to lift her tree-stump leg? I was front and center and there was a distinct odor emanating from her pussy. *Oh God, PLEASE don't make her bend over!* I didn't know about the other kids in class since they were art majors and used to this shit. But as for me, *I was out of there.* I'd rather have some sniper shooting at me in Viet Nam than have to look at this broad's fat ass for one more minute. I packed up my stuff and walked out of the classroom. *Fuck it.* I dropped the course and enrolled in some boring *statistics* course instead.

Space Ranger Gary the Burnout saw me and asked how the art class was going. I told him about my horrible experience with the fat girl and he said, *"No, man, they have different models every week. Most of the models are gorgeous women."* I did not believe Gary. He spent the major portion of his day acquiring, ingesting, snorting, smoking or shooting drugs. He was probably hallucinating. The entire thing was probably a figment of his drug-soaked imagination. Still, my curiosity got the better of me and I returned to the art class the next week. There in front of the room was the most devastatingly beautiful woman I had ever seen and she was stark naked. I sat in my seat, front and center sans my drawing materials and the professor asked me why I was there. *"I'm in this class,"* I said. "No, you're not," said Professor Killjoy, "you dropped the course." Oh, man. This loser is going to stand on formality when there's a naked angel standing on that pedestal. *"Well, can't I re-enroll?"* I asked. He said he was sorry but now the class was fully enrolled. *FUCK!!!!* The great thing about models is that they don't speak. I blew a chance to ogle a beautiful, sexy girl almost every week, have sex with her in my mind, and would not have to listen to her because she didn't say a word.

It wasn't my fault. I reacted to the moment. The stupid art professor should have stacked the deck and led with the angel not the heifer. It wasn't Space Ranger Gary's fault. He had been correct, for once in his life. He actually based a comment on fact. No, it was the dumbass dead guidance counselor's fault. He's the one who talked me out of going to a music conservatory. At that moment, I wished more than anything else that the hot shit recently deceased high school guidance counselor was alive again so I could kill him. *Bruciare all'inferno, bastardo! (Burn In Hell, Bastard!)*

The Dean Of Discipline

I am acquainted with a lot of really intelligent people, folks who truly possess remarkable abilities to understand the most obscure and dense principles relating to quantum mathematics, physics, curved space, philosophy, psychology, economics and business. But the more I am around these brilliant scholars, the more I am reassured by another firm belief of mine: the most perfect thing about life is its imperfection. That's not to say one should not try to be as good as one can be at a chosen endeavor. It's just to say that absolute perfection is not only impossible to achieve, it's a waste of time to attempt. Plus, it's boring. We are imperfect. But to quote the Bible again, "*Though we are sinners, God shows us His love always*." (***Romans 5:8)*** It takes a hell of a lot of pressure off us to realize this simple truth: We can only do our best, imperfect as our best may be.

This brings to mind an event that took place on April 1, 1965, my 15th birthday. As I walked to the subway station after another grueling day of high school, a friend of mine asked if he could borrow my train pass. He had forgotten his at home and had no money for the fare. *"Sure,"* I said, as we descended the steps that led to the turnstiles. My pal waited as I went through and flashed my train pass to the transit policeman stationed on the other side, checking to make sure we each possessed the little rectangular piece of cardboard that said our fares were paid a month in advance. Once inside, I slid my train pass inside a textbook that I was carrying and flung it back over the turnstile. "*Hey, man, you forgot your book,"* I yelled to my friend. I say again, we are imperfect creatures. Next thing I knew, my buddy and I were seated on a bench, the objects of everyone's curious looks, the transit cop pacing back and forth in front of us as if he had just nabbed Jesse James and Billy the Kid. After a moment of "thought", Mr. Transit Policeman confiscated my train pass and said that both my pal and I would be receiving *J.D. cards*. I wondered to myself, "*What the hell is a J.D. card?"* We asked the Transit Policeman what that meant. The transit cop sneered at us, "*J.D.* stands for *Juvenile Delinquent Card*." Quiet, shy, obedient, polite, humble little me, Breezie Ventura's son Trouble, was now officially a juvenile delinquent. And I would be the infamous possessor of my very own *Juvenile Delinquent Card.*

The Transit Policeman, doing his best impersonation of Elliot Ness, said, *"You know of course that these cards are given only to future criminals who will be watched closely by the authorities!"*

How could this be? How could I end up being a juvenile delinquent complete with a J.D.card? I'm such a nice kid. This is a little too imperfect. My mind was racing. My *birthday* and I'm getting a *damned J.D. card*! I was sure that I had just taken my first steps down the road to hell. I was sure that the cops were going to arrest me right there, before I even had any birthday cake. I was even surer that the Dean of Discipline at my high school was going to crucify me when I got to school next morning. After the transit cop was finished intimidating us, he allowed us to board the next train for home. He said he wouldn't "run us in" tonight but that the Dean of Disciple at our high school would deal with us in the morning. When the train pulled into the station, I walked home, head hung low. I was shaking and scared sick. I knew that my parents would not be bothered by such stupidity. My father wasn't exactly an angel. I was absolutely petrified by the thought of what the Dean of Discipline would do to a bona fide juvenile delinquent when he got his mitts on one.

I opened the front door of my house and there was Mom. *"What's wrong?"* she said. She expected me to explode through the door on my birthday, but I kind of slithered in. I was sure that juvenile delinquents slithered. I told her the story about the Great Train Pass Caper, the transit policeman, the Dean of Discipline and the juvenile delinquent card. I didn't expect her to freak out and she didn't. But she was upset because I was upset. She certainly wasn't angry with me. So she and I and my sister spent a quiet, somber hour or so waiting for my Pop to come home. When he did, he, like my mom, expected me to be bouncing off the walls. My mom and Pop threw a great birthday party and we were going to party tonight. *"Why so glum, boy?"* Pop asked. I told him the story. My pop listened attentively and when I finished my tale of woe, he gave me a true pearl of wisdom, not academic wisdom, but a heartfelt, sincere, very personal brand of folk wisdom that he possesses. My pop's untutored wisdom means more to me than all the "wisdom" of all the pompous, arrogant, self-important, pseudo-officious, semi-obscurantist hair-splitters in the world rolled into a snobby wad. My pop said to me:

"If that's the worst thing you're ever going to do in your life, do it again."

That little bit of true street wisdom set my heart at ease, cooled me out, made me smile, chased my fears away and made every lovely bite of my big, beautiful, chocolate birthday cake even more scrumptious. The next morning when I left for school, I asked my dad, "Will you and Ice Pick Sammy come to school with me and kill the Dean of Discipline for me?" Pop said to me, *"Don't worry. Go about your business as usual. Nothing bad is going to happen to you."* I thought to myself, *"The Fix is in!"* So I went to school. I didn't see the Dean of Discipline until after third period. I was walking to homeroom and spotted him walking down the hall, straight toward me. My blood ran cold and I felt nauseous. I was hoping my Pop had whacked this guy by now. I braced myself. But nothing happened. The Dean of Discipline passed me with the force of a freight train and he didn't even look at me. Our paths crossed twice more that day with the same result. I found this puzzling. Perhaps Dad met with him to *"explain"* the consequences of fucking with me?

After school, I played in a baseball game against one of the other high schools. I was not a great outfielder but I could hit the long ball. That afternoon, the pitcher threw a total of three fastballs to me over three times up at bat. I tattooed all three pitches for home runs, including the game winner. After the game, as I packed my equipment into my gym bag, I felt that someone was staring at me. I looked up and there was the Dean of Discipline and he was *smiling*. He reached out and *shook my hand*. "Great game," he said, "I don't think that last ball you hit has landed yet." Then the Dean of Discipline invited me to stop by his office anytime to check out his autograph collection. He had signed baseballs by Mickey Mantle, Roger Maris, and all the Yankees. He was a huge baseball fan and loved the

Yankees. So the fact that one of his students might possibly be good enough to win a college scholarship for baseball and maybe even get a chance to play professional baseball was a source of pride to him. I thought to myself, Pop must have got to this guy. When I got home, I told my Pop that the Dean of Discipline didn't even notice me in the hallway that afternoon. My revelations continued: I hit three home runs and the Dean of Discipline actually shook my hand after the game.

"How did you know everything would be OK, Pop? Did you threaten that arrogant scumbag?" I asked.

He smiled and said: *"I knew the transit cop wouldn't report such a minor thing to his boss. He isn't looking for more paperwork to do at the end of his shift. He wanted to scare you. He's a fucking pussy. He couldn't make it as a real cop so he became a transit cop. Fuck him. By the way, there is no such thing as a juvenile delinquent card."*

So my Pop knew the Dean of Discipline would not even find out about the Great Train Pass Caper. Pop said that I should dread nothing in life, because dreading something will make it so. I have followed his advice ever since. The Dean of Discipline and I actually became friends. I took him up on his offer to check out his autograph collection and he even gave me a baseball autographed by Yogi Berra. We sat discussing baseball for hours at a time. The Dean of Discipline and I had formed a bond. He wasn't a snobby scumbag after all. My dad, the Dean of Discipline, Ice Pick Sammy, and a few of the other guys and I even went to a bunch of Yankees games together. That was a bit surreal. But I was glad that they had not whacked the Dean of Discipline after all. My pop said that if the Dean of Discipline hadn't gone into the priesthood, he'd have made a good mobster. He was scary enough to intimidate just about anyone.

It's odd the way life resolves itself.

My dad didn't even have to kill anyone.

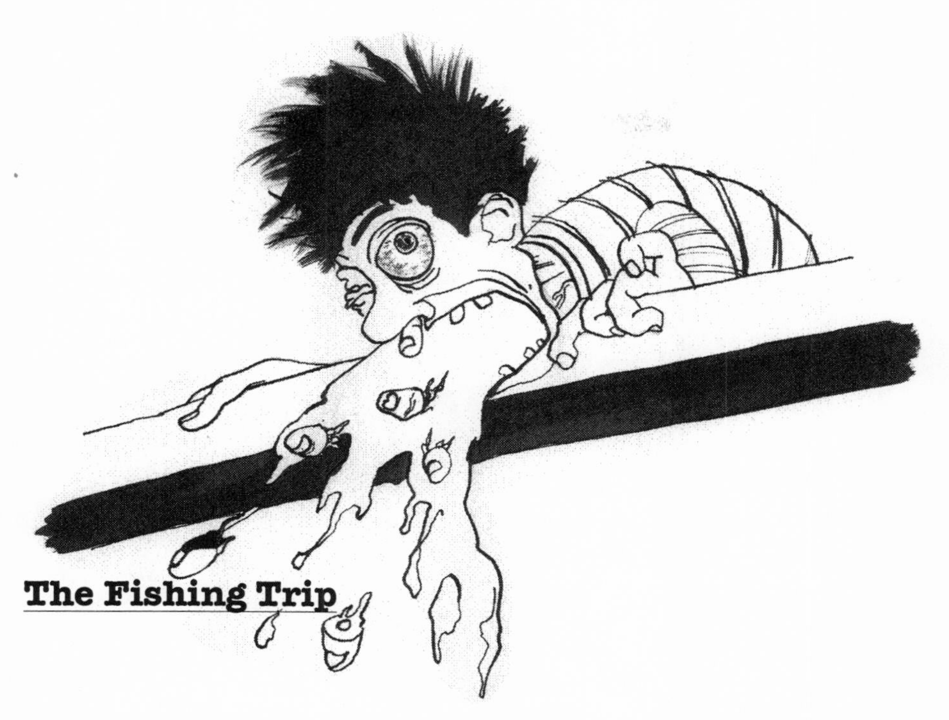

The Fishing Trip

I've always hated fishing. I don't eat fish. I don't want to hook them and haul them from their natural milieu. I don't want to touch them. In short, I hate to fish. But I love my dad and my dad loves to fish. Dad went fishing regularly with his crew: Ice Pick Sammy, Louie Blue Shoes, Bobby Goggles, Sweet Willie, Fat Patsy and Jimmy Cricket were just a few of the characters with whom Dad ran. They'd charter a boat and load it with beer, wine and Italian hero sandwiches like veal cutlet parmesan, eggplant parmesan, chicken cutlet parmesan and various Italian cold cut combos. They'd get up at 4 o'clock in the morning and drive out to Montauk. They had their favorite captain, some salt-encrusted skipper who smelled like shit and fish guts, and they'd meet him at 8AM sharp. Off they would go into the choppy waters off Block Island. Those guys were all veterans, believe it or not, and had been to sea in the Navy. The ocean was my father's second home. He didn't get seasick and neither did his friends. I, on the other hand, got seasick looking at the ocean on TV. I loved to swim but preferred the controlled environment of a swimming pool. Nothing heaved to and fro. Nothing would come surging up from the dark depths and rip my leg off (unless my sister was in a pissed off mood). As many times as my dad asked me to go fishing with him, I refused. At that point in my life, I still wanted to be a mobster. I wanted to kill people and make them cower at the sight of me. I wanted to be rich, spending millions of dollars that I'd made by being a gangster, doing all the illegal stuff that gangsters do. I wanted to be king of the world, but only on terra firma. I did not see myself as king of the ocean. On the ocean I was a pussy.

But one day, my dad, *"Mr. Tough-Guy-Mobster-I'll-Kill-The-Motherfucker & Then-Finish-My-Spaghetti,"* used a word he rarely used: *please*. I couldn't believe it. He seemed vulnerable at that moment, almost fragile. He called me into the living room and said that he and the guys were going fishing in the morning and would I please go with them. It would mean so much to him. The other guys bring their sons and he just misses me so much when he's out there on the water. As much fun as he has, it's not the same without me. I thought he was bullshitting me but I could see that he really meant it. Before I knew what was happening I heard myself say, "Sure, Dad, if it means that much to you." Now I've done some dumb-ass things before and since, but nothing I've ever done, including marrying my first wife, comes remotely close to this. I don't know what I was thinking. All the guys would be there and there'd be lots of yummy food and an ice chest filled with Coca-Cola just for me (everyone else drank beer and wine). The weather was supposed to be beautiful. Hell, it'll be good for me to get away for a day. *Who the fuck was I kidding*? I was in for a nightmare on the Atlantic Ocean and I knew it. I spent the next several hours alternating between calling myself a stupid fuck and trying to come up with an excuse my father would buy. But a favorite saying of my dad's was, "*Don't bullshit a bullshitter.*" I knew there was no way that I was getting out of this fishing trip. I couldn't sleep so I just stayed up, watched the Late, Late Movie on TV and waited for 4AM to roll around. It was like waiting to be executed.

Dad told me, as we all drove out to Montauk in a van, to always look at the horizon when on the water. That would prevent me from getting seasick. Plus one of the guys gave me Dramamine. That was also supposed to prevent me from getting seasick. But I entertained no illusions. I was on a drive to a fate worse than death. I was going to be bounced around the ocean like a cork in the waves. There would be no fun, no food and no laughter. There would be only that smelly captain, his inbred, toothless, pig-fucking first mate and miles of ocean. Amidst all the jokes the guys were telling in the van on the ride to Montauk and amidst all of their heartfelt assurances that I would not get seasick, I knew, nonetheless, that a watery doom awaited me. We finally pulled up to the docks and entered the parking lot. The boat was all stocked with fishing poles, bait, gaffing hooks, and even rifles. I asked Captain Smell-Like-Shit why we needed a rifle on a fishing trip. He said, "In case we catch a shark." *In Case We Catch A Shark?* "I don't get it," I said to him. "Well, young feller, if one o' dem big ol' Makos shake free from the hook when we get him on deck, he'll bite your leg off. So we just try to shoot the sum bitch before he get a chance to rip into ya." That was comforting.

"Yep," added the toothless inbred first mate, "A mean ol' Hammerhead took two o' my fangers." *"What in hell is a Fanger?"* I asked. The stupid fuck held up his left hand. His ring and pinky fingers were gone. I said to him, "*Oh, you mean fingers.*" He replied, "That's what I said, fangers." *"Well, why didn't you shoot him first?"* I asked. "We did," said the first mate, "but Skipper missed." He showed me several bullet holes in the deck.

I thought to myself, *You are officially fucked.*

As the boat started the two-hour trek to the fishing "grounds" (fishermen call the waters that yield good fishing, "grounds"…that too, I did not find comforting), the waves slammed against the side of the 100-foot vessel. I could feel the dizziness slowly descend upon me. I stared at the horizon. I dropped a Dramamine. I prayed. I didn't eat or drink anything. I prayed some more. I lay down on a bench. I sat up. I stood up. I paced on the deck. I tried to be one of the guys. But it was clear to everyone, especially *Captain Deadeye* and his first mate, *3-Fangers*, that I was in for a rough day. The sun was beating down on us and even the sombrero that I was wearing did little to shelter me from its intense rays. I felt like I was dying.

The first wave of nausea hit me the minute the boat stopped. We had arrived at the fishing grounds and the guys were ready to fish and party. "Trouble," Ice Pick Sammy said, "you have to eat. You'll get sicker if you have nothing in your stomach." I loved Sammy, but that was just about the worst advice I had even been given in my life. I downed a can of Coke and an eggplant sandwich. For a second, I actually felt better but then Mount Vesuvius erupted in my belly. I bolted for the rail and up came my lunch. Sammy and Dad held me so that I didn't go over the side as I puked. The water was so rough that when I was over the railing vomiting, waves were splashing my face. At times, my head was under water. I was in a state of animated suspension. It was as if this was not happening to me. It was as if I were watching it from outside my body. When I stopped puking, I tried to sleep but the rocking of the boat gave me a migraine headache. "Young feller," *Captain Dumbass* said. I opened my eyes into the blinding sun. "Why don't you come on up to the wheelhouse?" he asked. He had a big, comfy couch up there. It'd be much more comfortable than the wooden bench on which I now reclined. "OK, that might be good," I mumbled as I wobbled up the stairs. There was indeed a big comfy couch up there. Of course, it smelled like farts, fish and beer, but it was better than baking in the hot sun. Physics then became part of the equation. I should have known. The boat rocks even more up top than down on the deck. Pretty soon I added puke to the list of smells that the couch held.

I could not sleep, tired as I was, so I went back down to the deck. I once again donned my sombrero and tried with all I had left in me to be one of the guys. I picked up a fishing pole, the first mate put some bait on it, and I clicked the reel open. The sinker took the baited hook to the bottom, though it took a long time, and then I sat and waited, dizzy, disgusted and damned. Not five minutes passed when my fishing pole almost bent in half. The remaining line went whizzing off the reel. First Mate Fangers yelled to me, "You got something' big. Reel that sum bitch in." *You want me to reel it in?* I was hoping it didn't reel *me* right out of the boat. Everybody stopped their partying and ran over. They all cheered me on and for a moment I forgot how sick I was feeling. After almost a half hour of a brutal game of Tug of War, I pulled the thing from the water. It was a tiger shark and it was pissed. The skipper and the mate gaffed it in the gills and yanked it on the deck. The five-foot-long shark began snapping its vise-like jaws in every direction. It was every man for himself and all the half-drunk mobsters ran like scared little kids. They laughed as they ran, but they ran. I was way too sick and tired to move quickly but my dad grabbed me by the arm. He pulled me out of the way just as the shark lunged at my leg. The damned thing bit my fishing pole in half, bit a chunk out of the bench on which I had been sitting and (this was the funniest thing that I had witnessed all day) bit *First Mate Fangers* on his other hand. The tiger shark severed the ring and pinky fingers on his right hand. The skipper took out his rifle and dispatched the shark with three bullets to the head.

What a stroke of luck for me. My prayers had been answered. We had to cut the trip short and head back to port. We had to get the first mate to the hospital. He was screaming in pain. "I owe you guys another fishing trip, on me," said the Captain as he ran up the stairs to the wheelhouse. In a flash, the boat was racing for Montauk. My dad and Sammy wrapped *First Mate Stupid's* hand with bandages after disinfecting it with whiskey. But his fingers were in the shark's belly. I didn't give a hot shit where his fingers were. All I knew was that I had prayed for God to end this trip ASAP, in any way necessary, in any way possible. And God answered my prayers, albeit at the cost of a couple of digits.

I say to thee: the Lord works in mysterious ways.

The Registration Station

While the majority of time that I spent with my father was done so partaking in really fun-filled, albeit illegal, activities, we did share a few traditional father-son moments together. Dad was a big supporter of the United States Military. He was a veteran of World War II and served with distinction. I wear a ring he made from a shell casing. I keep his uniform preserved immaculately, cleaned and pressed in my closet. Yet, my dad did not want me to join the military and was certainly not in favor of the draft. He was staunchly opposed to the war in Viet Nam and did not want his son fighting an unseen enemy in the jungles of Southeast Asia. Unfortunately, my father had no connections to the top military people. This was one of the few agencies in the country to which my dad was not connected. To the U.S. Military, Domenico Ventura was simply an honorably discharged veteran who served from 1944-1945. When my military registration notice arrived by mail in 1968, Dad was not happy. But like so many other fathers of that era, he dutifully drove me to the army registration center to fill out the paperwork. Once done, it would only be a matter of time before Uncle Sam sent a letter ordering me to report for a physical examination.

Dad was unusually quiet as we drove to the registration station. I suppose I still had not digested the full import of the possibilities awaiting me should I be drafted. My dad did, that was obvious. This was one of the few times that we went anywhere alone together. We usually had at least a few more guys with us. It was a thing with my father: he never sat in a restaurant with his back to the door and he never went anywhere alone (or with only me). It was a rare occasion that he broke his personal rules and it made me nervous that this trip to the registration station was deemed such an occasion. He spoke little, but what he did say was deep. Although not directly relating to war and the prospect of my being drafted to fight in one, his musings were genuinely heartfelt:

"I wouldn't want to live anymore if anything ever happened to you. This thing I've built is for you. Someday, you will be Re Del Mondo (King of

the World). This I promise."

This wasn't your usual father & son, birds & bees type talk. Dad was setting me up with my own crew, my own family. He was teaching me to be a *Don,* and the military, which he revered, was not part of the plan.

We arrived where the registration took place, and Dad parked the car in the lot across the street. He was looking at this crumbling structure as if it were the Empire State Building and he was a dirt farmer from Iowa sightseeing in The Big Apple for the first time. Dad had a funny way of looking up: he shaded his eyes, his mouth slightly agape, and mumbled almost inaudible figures and thoughts out loud. He was thinking. This set off an alarm in my head. The registration station was four stories high and built in the late 19th century. It had seen its better days. I think a strong wind might have blown it over. But my father, from across the street, sized it from the ground up to the roof. We entered through the once-regal gold doors. These too had seen their better days and now they were dirty, lop-sided and falling off their hinges. As we walked up the stairs and through the corridors, my father kept knocking on the walls, as one might knock on the front door of a house when calling on a friend. He stamped his feet on the floors and his ever-calculating mind was working overtime. What on earth was he thinking? There is no one here deserving to die. Why would he whack a military clerk? He loved the military and the fact that I had just turned 18, thus becoming eligible for military service wasn't the clerk's fault. Not even a *Don* would order such a hit. Patsy would talk Dad out of that for sure. No, there was something cooking in my father's brain but murder wasn't it.

The person in charge was a very sweet black lady, a Corporal in the army. She could see that my father was not happy with the possibility of me being drafted and sent to Viet Nam. She and Dad talked for a long time. She was sincerely kind to us and my dad appreciated that. I have no doubt that he, in some way, repaid her for comforting us and for taking care of the registration as quickly as possible. There was a giant file cabinet behind her desk. It contained thousands of index cards. The registration station had not yet been computerized. Nothing was in duplicate. My paperwork and index card were filed in a folder with my name on it. She placed the folder in the drawer and that was it. Dad asked if he could use her telephone and she said, "Sure." I don't know whom my father called but within minutes a dozen red roses were delivered to the Corporal and enough food to feed an army (no pun intended), was served to the entire staff. We actually stayed and ate lunch with everyone there. The Corporal seemed genuinely fond of my father and he saluted her when we left.

Just before we departed, Dad asked the Corporal: "*Will anyone be here tomorrow?"*

The Corporal replied: *"No. The building is closed on the weekends."* The next day was Saturday.

Dad thanked her again and we were off.

I thought my father asked her that particular question because he was planning on coming back to take her to lunch the next day, if the registration station was open. Those two definitely took an instant liking toward one another. But my dad's nefarious mind works on its own schedule and flirting was not his priority at this point. He had something far more sinister brewing.

My father woke me up at 6AM on Saturday morning and said, *"Get dressed, boy, we have to go do a thing."* This was a common occurrence in my life. There was always a "thing" to do: pick up money, break a guy's leg, murder a guy, dispose of a body, etc. I gave it no thought whatsoever. I showered, ate a yummy breakfast that Dad cooked for me, got dressed and we left. We stopped at my Godfather's house to fetch him. Uncle Zoot, dapper as always, jumped into the front seat as I hopped into the back.

"What do you say, Kid?" Zoot asked, a big smile on his face. *"How's it hanging?"*

"Zoot," Dad said, *"Did you make that phone call?"*

Uncle Zoot answered that he had, as Dad began to drive.

"Good. Let's go watch," Dad said.

Zoot practically went through the roof, *"Wait a while, wait a while. We can't go there now. There's no need! It's going to happen. Non ti preoccupare. (Don't worry.)*

My father said, *"I want to see it, Zoot. It'll be fun."*

I had no idea what these two maniacs had planned but something was going to happen and Dad wanted to watch. So we drove off to an as-yet-undisclosed destination.

You can imagine my surprise when we parked across the street and down the block from the registration station. What was going on? The place is closed! My dad had Uncle Zoot and me puzzled. As far as Uncle Zoot was concerned, he had pushed a button, "Do such-and-such at such-and-such address." He was flabbergasted when he realized the location.

Before I could put two thoughts together, an explosion such as I had never witnessed actually rocked our car. The registration station was blown off the face of the Earth. Everything inside was incinerated. It was as if the building had become a blast furnace. Nothing remained. The file cabinets melted. The thousands of index cards, containing the names of we who just became eligible for military service, were gone.

My father was always miles ahead of the trend in technology. Primitive as they may seem today, computers were in use in the 1960s and my dad, Zoot and a number of the other mob guys were very much aware of state of the art. They knew the possibilities and were even a bit ahead of the curve.

Dad said to Zoot wryly, *"Index cards. No computers, no backup systems, not even carbon copies!"*

Zoot roared with laughter, *"Holy fucking shit!"*

It did not stop the military draft effort in its tracks but it threw a wrench into the works. It was several months before that particular registration station was up and running again.

Dad smiled as the building burned. Intense and furiously hot blue and yellow flames shot hundreds of feet into the air. Smoke filled the sky. It was chaos.

My father looked at me, with the most loving look I had ever seen him give anyone, and said, *"Happy birthday, Son."*

If You Want To Learn About Sin

My father lies in a bed in a nursing home, unable to get up, unable to eat without help, unable to take care of the everyday personal tasks to which humans must tend. I have seen him reduce human beings to bloody mounds of rotting waste. I used to love to watch Dad kill people. They'd crap in their pants, literally, as he split their skulls open. It made me proud to be his son. *Nobody fucked with my father.* I always thought my dad would either live forever or go out in a hail of bullets, taking 100 cops with him. I watch him now struggle to remember my name, barely able to think, unable to move. It kills me. I revere him. I regret that I wasted so many years trying to fit into a bullshit "normal" society where the reward for sacrifice is more sacrifice and the reward for suffering is more suffering. In the world into which I was born, there was no sacrifice or suffering. *We were kings.* Fuck everybody else. It was how we lived for a long, long time. I thought we'd always live that way. But I learned that the future is unpredictable. That was a harsh lesson. Now I see my dad as he lies helplessly in his bed. I wonder: *Am I looking at myself? Does the Alzheimer's that has destroyed his body and mind run in the bloodline? Am I the next to fall to this vile disease?*

Dad had a saying: *If you want to learn about sin, ask a sinner, not a priest.* Sinning was my dad's specialty. He ran with the devil and fucked the devil's daughter. He made no excuses. If you didn't like it, *fuck you.* It was somewhat startling to see my dad in church on Sunday mornings, worshipping God, donating money to the poor, helping with numerous community projects, cooking bacon and eggs at the Father & Son Communion Breakfasts and coaching the Little League baseball team on which I played. All the while, he was stealing, cheating, pimping, bookmaking and murdering. It was an odd paradox. Even at the age of 12, I thought this was an odd paradox. Don't misunderstand. I didn't think any less of my dad. To the contrary, I held him in even higher esteem. *He is the man! He has the fucking world conned.* I adopted this lifestyle at an early age. I learned from the best. I became very skilled in the fine arts of deception and persuasion. I learned how to lie and cheat by observing Dad. He took me everywhere with him. I've seen him kill a lot of people. He was a wild man. Dad would tear into guys, jamming his fingers into their eye sockets and ripping their skulls apart. I *loved* to watch him do that. I had absolutely no regard for human life. As long as Dad, Patsy, the crew and I were on the streets, I was happy. *Fuck everybody else.* When I was younger and the guys had a bunch of call girls come to *The Little Shop of Insanity*, I wasn't allowed to be in the bedrooms. They were upstairs. At 10 years of age, I didn't know what was happening anyway. But I had to stay downstairs in the parlor and watch the baseball game on television. As I grew older, however, Dad added a bedroom just for me. It was an amazing time in my life. I was becoming as violent and cunning as my father and he was proud of me. When I was 13 years old, grown men would cross the street when they saw me. They knew that I was *The Don's* son. They knew I could gut them with one swipe of my Bowie knife and then disappear into the shadows. They didn't want any part of me and I liked it that way. The fact that I never killed anyone still bothers me and astonishes me. As I have said, The Lord intervened every time. The plan that I respect, other than my own, is The Lord's master plan. I don't mess with The Lord. I see now, at age 60, why my dad always honored God. The Creator is the only one who can take us down.

Still, I have always wished that I had been given the opportunity to rip a guy's skull apart. It isn't like playing God. I see now that even Dad did not consider himself on a par with God, but it was the next best thing. I look back with pride and satisfaction upon all the dastardly things that I have done. I have caused a great deal of damage in my life. I have evened the score with a good many jerk-offs who dared fuck with me. I have desecrated corpses, maimed people and ran with thieves. I could steal the eyes right out of your head and you wouldn't know it until you walked into a wall. But I have never killed anyone.

In a lot of ways, I ran my con the same as Dad. I was an altar boy who would steal anything in the church that wasn't too big for me to carry. I would lie to the nuns and tell them I was serving mass and lie to the Priests and tell them I was in school. Then I'd go smoke weed with my friends. I made more money at age 16 than most grown men made working full-time jobs to support their families. I was *loaded*. I was running my game and having a *good* time.

I've always hated *weak shit.* Today weak shit is the younger generation that thinks it's cool because it has a certain haircut or wears a certain shirt or listens to bullshit pop music. Weak shit is anything that is bullshit, anyone that is bullshit. It takes all my will power not to fucking slaughter the little scumbags that swear they're cool. We live in pathetic times. In today's global bullshit society, the only people that I truly revere are the soldiers who put it all on the line to preserve our freedom. You *cannot* test them. They trump me, no contest. I thank God for them. Other than the military, it's all weak shit if it's part of the popular culture. My dad taught me to live outside that bizarre world.

If you want to learn about sin, ask a sinner. Although my dad met his match in The Lord, it is only The Creator who has the power to take him down. I am still proud to be his son. I know that the wisdom, savvy and savagery I have inherited from him will take me far. I am no longer interested in playing by anyone's rules but my own. I am comforted to know that when I am finally taken down, it will only be by God.

Girls Who Puked On Me

I am trying not to take this personally: for some reason, girls often puke in my presence. It's been happening all my adult life. I shower every day and I use deodorant. I even rub patchouli in my shoes. But the girls continue to puke - not only in my presence, *on me*. Now I don't care what contemporary beauty you name, she's going to lose her sex appeal after blowing chunks on your sneakers. They get all squishy and they smell awful. I can find nothing sexy with that. Forget about a boner: *Down Periscope*. Plus you have to throw the sneakers away. And no matter how many showers you take after that, the malodorous remnants are not easy to kill off, to say nothing of the bruised ego and horrifying cerebral reruns through which one must subject oneself. I'm not even including the little girls who puked on me when I was a kid. Kids puke. No big deal. That didn't bother me. It's the women whom I have dated and yes married who are the subjects of this little ode.

As such, let's start at age 18. It is June 1968, my senior class boat trip up the Hudson River to Rye Beach, NY. Theoretically, we're adults, 18 years old, about to graduate high school. We're cruising up the Hudson from lower Manhattan on a beautiful late spring day. There were about 200 of us on board. The boat was big, stable and sturdy. It barely rocked as it cleaved through the water. If Manhattan Island wasn't slowly drifting by, you wouldn't even know you were on the river. The trip to Rye took about two hours, during which the kids ate BBQ hot dogs, burgers, fries and even ribs. We got to Rye Beach, sun shining, and we hit the rides. The thing is, most of the kids had full bellies. Not me. I always hated meat. I was fine riding the roller coaster repeatedly. It seemed most of the others were OK too. Most 18 year olds have iron stomachs. After a few hours of rides, more eating and baking in the midday sun, it was time to board the boat and head back to Manhattan. My girlfriend, Christine, and I were dancing to the sounds of Jimi Hendrix, The Who and all the great bands of the day when the sky suddenly turned dark. The wind came up and the water got a bit choppy. It didn't bother me at all. I hadn't eaten much all day. It wasn't a hurricane;

it was just windy and bumpy on the water. I was digging it. Occasionally, the boat would rock from side to side, as a wave would slam against us. As the weather went from bad to worse, so did Christine's stomach. She was a beauty, blonde hair, blue eyes, intelligent, funny, kind, loving and now sick as a dog. The Beach Boys' "Surfer Girl" chimed over the stereo system and I held Christine in my arms as we danced. I asked if she was OK and she said she was, although she looked a bit ashen to me. She rested her head on my shoulder and for a brief minute it was one of the romantic moments of my life. I was just about to whisper, "I love you," when I felt her back heave in my arms and a gush of lumpy liquid ooze down my shirt. The funkiest smell I ever had the misfortune to inhale waft up my nostrils and down my throat. Christine had puked down my back and fainted. My shirt was saturated with this disgusting substance that was dripping down to my ass by now, from inside my shirt. The priests and nuns came running over (we went to a Catholic high school), took her from my arms and carefully laid her down on the deck. The Captain was right there with smelling salts and the nurse (we always took a nurse with us on field trips for just such a situation) soon had Chris up and about. But I smelled like shit. The Captain took me up to the wheelhouse and gave me a T-Shirt with the boat's name on it. I went into the bathroom and washed as best I could. Christine even washed my back – it was her puke after all. The Captain sprayed Lysol on me but it could have been Raid. Nothing helped. I reeked all the way home. Only one person got sick on that trip, my girlfriend. And only one person got puked on, me.

Then there was Francesca. She was so beautiful and funny I knew she had to be too good to be true. And she was. Francesca was fun-loving and sweet. She was a good person. She had only one problem. At age 18, she was a full-blown alcoholic. I had a huge crush on her. My cousin told me that Francesca thought I was cute and that she would go out with me. "With me?" I asked. I felt like Charlie Brown when he got invited to the Halloween party. But it was true. Francesca told my cousin that she'd go out with me if I asked her. So I did. And she said, "Yes!" My cousin & her boyfriend came along with us and we went to that old standby, Rye Beach. This was the same place where my last adventure in *Vomitville* happened. We picked up Francesca and as she got into the car I could detect the faint odor of alcohol layered with copious amounts of mouthwash. I didn't think much of it except when she would burp under her breath. Then the liquor topped the mouthwash. Still, she was coherent and funny and so damned cute. When we got to Rye Beach, Francesca started banging back the brews, which she took from a cooler she brought. She also brought some yummy eggplant parmesan sandwiches that she made and which we all ate with great enthusiasm. Francesca looked stunning in a bikini. She was perfect. That's all I can say. She was petite, brunette, cuddly and gorgeous, with a smile that lit up the world and made the sun look like an amateur in illumination. I could see myself falling in love with her, marrying her, starting a family with her and spending the rest of my life with her. What I didn't see was the amount of alcohol she was consuming. Beer was followed by tequila, and that was followed by rum. All I ever drank was Coca-Cola. To this day I have never had a drink in my life. At that moment, sitting on the golden sand, basking in the glorious sun, Francesca was doing enough drinking for the both of us. But she remained in control, laughing at my stupid jokes, holding my hand, walking along the seashore. She gave no hint that she was absolutely stone cold drunk. I was clueless. We came upon a bench and sat down, alone with our young, raging hormones. A gentle, warm sea breeze wrapped itself around us as we embraced. I was just about to kiss Francesca's full, lush lips when said, "Hold on just a minute." No sooner had those words left her mouth that a geyser of puke followed. She puked in Technicolor. She puked in the sand, on herself, on me, on the bench, even on a seagull that got a bit too close. When she finally stopped, she took a piece of bubble gum out of her beach bag and popped it in her mouth. "Now, where were we?" she asked. "Just going home," I said. That was the end of my extremely short-lived romance with Francesca. As we drove back to the City, where we lived, she slept with her head on my shoulder. Although every impulse in my soul told me to try to help her, to take care of her, to watch over her, my brain told me it was hopeless. I was 19 years old, a sophomore in college. I had barely tasted life. I was torn because I think I was in love with her. I hated myself for leaving her, for cutting off contact with her. But I knew that she would ultimately take me down. She was too far gone, at least for an immature kid like me. In the months that followed, I heard that she had gotten into pills and developed a horrible drug habit in addition to her alcoholism. Sometimes I would see her walking down the street. She was in a fog. She was still the cutest, most loveable girl I had ever seen. But now she walked like a junkie. As time went on, it got more difficult to hide. Until one day, she just disappeared. Someone told me she moved to California. Someone else told me she moved to England. I don't know what happened to her. She was simply gone. I still think of her, over 40 years later. I wish I had a witty way to end this part of the set. But the helplessness and guilt I felt when I abandoned her were not funny, young and immature as I was. I don't even know if she is still alive. My guess is that she died long ago. Nonetheless, I think I might still be in love with the adorable girl I took to Rye Beach in 1969 and with whom I spent the most magical afternoon of my life before or since.

By 1975, I was spending a good deal of my time on the road, playing bass with a variety of show bands, lounge bands and cover bands. It was the second tier below the Big Time. I would occasionally get to back up a shooting star, a one-hit wonder touring her/his smash record but for the most part I played in bar bands. I was, and am, a musician, a bass player. I make a good deal of my living playing my bass for money. The music didn't matter at that time. If you had the dime, I had the time, as the saying goes. I drove all over the country with bar bands, playing the hits of the day for barrooms full of drunken whores, topless dancers, cheaters, lost souls and characters of every description. On one particular stint at a third rate club in Miami Beach, I was playing in a disco band, doing my best to stay awake as I plunked out the bass line to "Fly Robin Fly" and other rather forgettable ditties. We were at the Casablanca Lounge for a Friday & Saturday stint with grueling 10PM until 4AM sets each night. On Saturday night I noticed a sexy, really hot girl dancing in front of me all night. She was smiling and winking at me. I really thought she was having a joke with me. This was not a normal occurrence in my life. At the time, I was 250 lbs. and sporting a full beard and long hair. I looked like a water buffalo in a sequined jumpsuit and platform shoes. But throughout the evening and into the wee hours she continued to flirt with me. At the end of the gig, I was packing up and she asked if she could come up to my room and hang out for a while. Well, that was the fastest I ever said the word *"sure"* in my life. She was drunk as a skunk but I didn't care. I just kept thinking to myself, I am going to score tonight, no doubt. (I have since stopped saying “no doubt” to myself.) I unlocked the door to my room and we sat on the couch. She said she was hungry but all I had to eat was popcorn. So I made a big bowl of the stuff, which she wolfed down in record time. At this point, although she was beginning to burn a rather frightening shade of green, she began to disrobe. Before I knew it, this gorgeous, green creature was naked and lying on top of me. She had phenomenal boobs, which she used to smother me. I was in heaven. We were about five minutes into our lust fest when she suddenly stopped and said, “I don’t feel so good.” After a night of drinking rum on an empty stomach and then bombarding her stomach with copious amounts of popcorn, it was little wonder. I was about to ask her if she wanted me to call the house doctor when she erupted. She puked on the couch, on the wall, on the table, on the rug, on herself and, yes, on me. I had gone from heaven to hell in a millisecond. I was beginning to get a bit tired of girls throwing up on me, too. As I sat on a couch covered in a multi-textured layer of bodily fluids and partially digested popcorn, it was obvious that I needed to do something to help her. I carried her to the bathroom where she deposited into the toilet the last remnants of an evening of partying. Then I put her and myself into the shower. I scrubbed her luscious yet disgusting body with soap with one hand and held her up with the other. Then I dried her off and put her in my bed. She was asleep before her head hit the pillow. At this point it was something like 5:30 in the morning and I was so tired I couldn’t even think about cleaning the room. It took me about two minutes to climb in bed next to her and nod off. Around noon, there was a knock on the door. I woke up and with a raspy voice asked, “Who is it?” “Housekeeping,” a young, perky voice answered. “May I come in to clean your room?” “Yes!” I replied, forgetting about the puke encrusted mess we had left in the living room. Well, I don’t know what language she was speaking but I am sure that this maid was not saying anything I’d repeat to my mom. I’m pretty sure she was calling me some nasty cuss words. I came running out of the bedroom in my robe, apologizing, helping her to clean up, begging her not to tell the management, when, fresh as a daisy and naked as a jaybird, my voluptuous friend walks past us and into the bathroom. “Morning,” she chirped. I’m pretty sure the maid used the “F” word in whatever language she was speaking. When she came out of the bathroom, my friend called room service and ordered a Bloody Mary, after which the maid called her boss. I had to pay for a professional cleaning service to *de-pukify* the room, so there went my entire weekend's paycheck. After she drank her breakfast, my friend gave me her number and asked me to call her later. But I had to make the 400-mile drive with the band to the next city and the next gig. I never did ask that girl her name. No matter. I had a feeling that she had many more nights of drinking and puking ahead of her and I wanted no part of it.

As I said earlier, there is absolutely nothing erotic or sexy about a girl, albeit a beautiful girl, puking on you. I have no idea why it happened to me with such regularity. But one thing is for sure, when (and if) I ever get to the Pearly Gates, I plan to ask God: *What Was Up With That*?

Fuck Bing Crosby

I don't want you to get the idea that everything was all shoot-them-up mob shit in the earlier years of my life. It wasn't. I dated girls, got married twice and, while I was no Don Juan, I did consider myself a romantic. There was a girl named Patty in the neighborhood and in 1977, I had recently gotten divorced from my first wife. I had been dating a number of women but no one moved me. Patty, on the other hand, was that special someone. I didn't even know her but every time I saw her I said, "She's the one." I was not shy around women. The timing was off. For a couple of years, I was married to my first wife. Later, when I was single again, Patty wasn't around. I didn't know where she lived exactly but I always had an eye out for her. One evening I finally saw her as she was leaving her house. The problem was that she jumped into a red Fiat Spider driven by some punk wannabe junior mobster. I ran towards the car, trying to catch up to it before they sped off. I wanted to ask Patty out on a date. If the dickhead behind the wheel would have said anything I would have slit his throat with my Bowie knife, which I carried in a sheath on my belt at all times. But I was not quick enough and they went off into the night. However, now I knew where she lived. I continued to date other women but I could think only of Patty. The other girls didn't like to do the things I enjoyed: great movies, museums, fine dining, music, and all the other cultural things that New York City offers. I wasn't looking for a quick fuck and "see you later." As I said, I was a romantic. I wanted someone with whom I could share life. I circled Patty's block for weeks with hopes of catching her entering or leaving her house. But she was a difficult one to catch.

Then one day I saw her as she was coming home from work. I walked up to her and said:

"Excuse me, I realize that you don't know me…"

She cut me off and said, "I know you. You're Trouble Ventura."

"Yeah," I said with a somewhat perplexed look on my face.

"I'm Marty's little sister, Patty."

"No way!" I said.

Marty and I went to high school together. But he went to college out of state after we graduated and I hadn't seen him in years. The last time I had seen his little sister, she was a kid. Now she was a grown woman of 23. I asked Patty for a date and she said, "Yeah, sure."

So the next night, I rang the doorbell of Patty's house sharply at 6PM. Patty answered the door and I knew I was staring at my soul mate. She was absolutely beautiful, with long red hair, freckled button nose and alabaster skin. I handed her a bouquet of a dozen red roses and she invited me in to meet her mom. As I entered the house I could hear the TV News on in the parlor. Patty introduced me to her mom just as the guy on TV said:

"Crooner and screen actor Bing Crosby died today."

Well, Crosby had been in the news for some time because it was learned that he had beaten his children when they were young. He was a strict disciplinarian, apparently, and used the strap on his kids with great regularity during their childhood. Having grown up with my dad, who was *not* a disciplinarian with me, I thought Crosby was a piece of shit for hitting his kids. I was trying to be on best behavior but out of nowhere I blurted:

"Fuck Bing Crosby. I'm glad the son of a bitch is dead."

An awkward silence followed. There were two things about Patty's mom I had yet to learn:

1) She did not tolerate cursing in her house and

2) She *LOVED* Bing Crosby.

So I had two strikes against me before we even left the house. Patty whispered the lowdown to me and I humbly apologized. "I'll let it go this once," she said, a slight albeit obvious smile on her lips. I could tell Patty's mom liked me. She was a witty, bright and very hip woman who passed away far too young. But she did live to see Patty and me get married. By this time

I was traveling a lot with a number of bands, trying to earn a meager living as a musician. It was difficult. Between hustling the occasional recording session and driving hundreds of miles every week to play everything from bars to Bar Mitzvahs, my stress levels were very high. All the while, Dad was saying, "You can come back to work with me anytime you want, boy." It was tempting. But I was determined to do music for a living. I had been seeing Patty for about a year, living in a little apartment in New York City and scraping out a living playing music. I was barely paying my bills but at least I was living on my own terms.

I have always acted on impulses and it was on such an impulse that I decided to ask Patty to marry me. I was with a friend of mine driving to Cleveland for a weekend set at a disco there. It's about a 10 to 12 hour drive with stops to eat, etc. We would be three days early because we had nothing else to do. I thought we'd see whatever sights there were to see in Cleveland. The disco we were playing had rooms for us so that was not a problem. The manager said we could drive out early. We'd been on the road about six hours. I was behind the wheel as my friend slept. I was suddenly overwhelmed with the urge to ask Patty to marry me. As I have mentioned a number of times, I am a romantic and a romantic asks a woman to marry him in person. So as my buddy slept, I turned the car around and headed back to New York. By the time he woke up, we were exactly where we were when he fell asleep. It was more or less near Scranton, PA.

He said, "Man, I thought I was asleep for hours but it must have been only a few minutes. We're still in Scranton."

I said, "No, man. I turned around near Youngstown, Ohio. We're heading back to New York."

"Why?" he asked. "Did the gig get cancelled?"

I explained that I intended to ask Patty to marry me, and a romantic does so in person, etc. *"Do you mean you turned around just to ask Patty to marry you? Ever heard of a device called a telephone?"* he hollered.

But my mind was made up. We were back in New York by 8AM. I

was driving to Patty's when I happened to see her walking to the subway to go to work. I honked the horn and waved.

"I thought you were in Cleveland for a gig?" she said.

I got out of the car, knelt on one knee in the middle of the street and asked her to marry me. "Yes, I'll marry you," she said. I was elated. "But why didn't you just call me instead of driving all the way back?" she asked.

"FUCKING ASSHOLE," my pal screamed at me from the car.

I didn't care. My soul mate was going to be my wife! To this day, if you mention this event to my friend, he goes nuts. Patty got on the subway and I got back in the car. "Let's go to Cleveland," I said. *"Fuck you,"* was the reply. My pal didn't speak to me until we got to Ohio. He was fuming mad. Then he broke his silence as we left Pennsylvania. "Congratulations," he said, "you lucky bastard." He smiled a big old smile and there was a tear in his eye.

When our wedding day rolled around my dad was in rare form. All of the City mob guys were in the banquet hall. I was betting the FBI had a surveillance van across the street. After the ceremony, my dad got the Justice of the Peace so drunk he pissed his pants. The judge was hanging with all these mob guys that he didn't know were mob guys. He became fast friends with my dad and Zoot. That friendship lasted until the judge's death (natural causes) many years later. God only knows what kind of illegal shit those two maniacs got the judge involved in. There was singing and dancing and all sorts of carrying on. Dad gave us a pocket full of money, Fat Patsy gave us a new car, Ice Pick Sammy, Smokey, Zoot, and a number of the other guys chipped in and bought us a house. I was in heaven. It was, and is, the happiest day of my life. Of all the blessings The Lord has bestowed on my unworthy ass, marrying Patty is blessing number one.

And it all started with a simple phrase: *Fuck Bing Crosby.*

This Man's Army

I remember my cousin Antonio saying something to me about a war that was happening in Viet Nam in 1967. We were in high school and I gave no thought whatsoever to politics and world affairs. We cared only about music and girls. We played in bands and tried to get dates with girls. Viet Nam could have been in… *ASIA* … for all we knew. I cannot even recall exactly what Antonio said that day in the subway. He simply mentioned that there was trouble in this Viet Nam place. I recall quite vividly, however, becoming extremely unsettled by his words. There was something ominous about them.

The next time I heard anything of Viet Nam was in 1968 when cousin Antonio was drafted into the Army. Everyone in our family was hoping that he wouldn't get sent to Viet Nam. But, of course, he was. He ended up getting wounded twice before they finally sent him home a year later. When he got back in 1969, he bought a Harley Davidson motorcycle and did wheelies up and down the street all the time. Cousin Antonio and I never once spoke about his experiences in Viet Nam although he wrote me a letter one time from right in the middle of the war zone. He said a guy in his platoon was always getting into trouble for failing to lace his combat boots. The Sergeant told him several times that this was a dangerous habit. Sure enough, one night, while on patrol, the fellow stepped out of his boot while crossing a muddy-bottomed river. When they got to the other side the guy realized he had no shoe on one foot. But they didn't carry spare boots so he had to walk barefoot. A few minutes later the guy was bitten on the side of his foot by a venomous snake. He died the next day. So I didn't get the impression that Antonio had a good time in Viet Nam. A lot of the guys Antonio and I grew up with went to Viet Nam and a few were killed over there as well. My area of New York was hit hard by that war.

When I was a junior at university, the Selective Service people had a lottery to see who would be the first to get called for military service. The year was 1971 and for some reason they had a lottery that year. They started with #1 and pulled a ping pong ball out of a spinning drum. The ball had a date on it. If that date was your birthday, your number was 1 and you were going to be called for the draft first. They went on down the line, #2, #3, #4, etc. If you got beyond #100 or so, you probably would not be called. But if your number was lower than 100, you were going to be called for the draft. All over the USA, people sat in front of their TV sets and watched this televised crapshoot with hopeful but heavy hearts. My family sat around the TV set too. Now I *never* won a game of chance in my life but of course *I won this damned lottery.* My number was 32. My mom cried, my girlfriend cried, my sister cried. My pop paced. I was too numb to do anything but stare at the TV. Friends began to treat me differently, especially those who had received high numbers therefore rendering them untouchable. They looked at me with sad eyes and spent more time with me than they normally would. They talked about "old" times even though we hadn't lived long enough to have "old" times. It came as no surprise to me that I received my draft notice on my birthday, April 1, 1972. I was to report to Whitehall Street for a physical examination a few weeks later.

I walked around in a stupor until the day of my physical exam arrived. That morning at 5AM, my pop walked into my room to wake me up but there was no need – I had not been able to sleep all night. I needed another pearl of wisdom from my Pop but was not certain that even he could find any hope on this dismal morning. I showered and drank a quick cup of coffee. I wasn't hungry so I skipped breakfast. My pop walked me to the front door, silent, as if walking me to my grave. As I opened the door and stepped outside, the sun was rising, the birds were singing. My Pop said, *"Keep the faith, Son. I had a talk with Il Capo Di Tutti Capi (the Boss of All Bosses) last night."* Pop was pointing to the heavens as he said this. *"I asked Him for a favor,"* Pop said. This gave me a tremendous sense of hope and well-being because I knew my pop had spent the night praying for me. I hugged him and headed off to the subway station. Oddly enough, I met a bunch of my friends on the train. We were all going to the same place, Whitehall Street. We were all going to our physical examinations and we were all praying that we would not be inducted into the Army and shipped out to Viet Nam in the weeks ahead.

Whitehall Street is in the lower part of Manhattan. That's where the Induction Center was at the time. As we walked from the subway station to the Induction Center, we realized that there was a virtual army of us, hundreds of kids, all heading there. I was nervous but I wasn't scared. I recalled my pop's words from years back: *Dread nothing. To dread a thing makes it so.* So I went with the flow. I noticed that a lot of guys had file folders in their hands, folders that contained charts, reports and a million reasons why the holder of this file should not be inducted into the military. I thought to myself, *"Shit. I should have taken some files with me, doctors' reports, something."* The first Army guy I met was sitting at a desk in the front hallway as I entered the building. I pulled my wrinkled draft notice from my pocket and handed it to him. He picked up a packet of paperwork in a manila envelope printed with *UNITED STATES MILITARY INDUCTION CENTER, WHITEHALL STREET* on the front. It also had *my name* on it. This made me a bit uncomfortable. He handed the packet to me. "Room 54," he said. He did not bark at me. He barked at every single guy who held a file folder of excuses. But he just said, "Room 54," to me, in a casual tone of voice. He even nodded in the direction of Room 54 to show me the way. I said, "Thank you, Sir," and he *smiled* at me. "You're welcome," he said. I knew my Pop was connected but this was ridiculous. Inside Room 54, I sat with all my friends. It was obvious that our room assignment was based on location of residence. All the guys from my neighborhood were going to be together for the entire examination. There were about 50 of us in Room 54, nervously chatting, when in walked the next Army guy I met. He was a Master Sergeant, big as an ox and tall as a tree, with clusters of medals pinned on his chest. When he spoke, it sounded like thunder. The first words he said to us were, *"Gentlemen, three weeks from now 95% of you will be in This Man's Army."* That meant that roughly one or two of us would receive a deferment and the other 48 or so would be going to Viet Nam. The paper shuffling was quite audible as file folders were being rifled all around me. Guys were getting all their reports, charts, graphs and doctors' notes in alphabetical order, color-coded, in triplicate. I had no file folder, just the packet of paperwork the Army guy at the front entrance gave me. It was at that point that I thought I might well end up getting inducted into the Army. I wasn't giving up hope. I was preparing myself for an eventuality that seemed to be the odds-on favorite. Then another weird thing happened. The Master Sergeant looked with obvious scorn at all the guys who had file folders and bellowed, *"I hate file folders."* Suddenly, I was really glad I didn't have a file folder and made damned sure the Master Sergeant saw that my hands were empty. The Master Sergeant growled: *"Everyone with a file folder, leave the damned thing on your desk and follow me."* The guys reluctantly left the folders behind and walked out into the hallway, as if a firing squad awaited them. But I had a feeling that the Master Sergeant was just trying to scare them and doing a damned good job. He walked back into Room 54 after the file folder guys were lined up outside. There were just two of us, a buddy of mine (whom I just met – you become instant friends with folks when you are in the Induction Center at Whitehall Street) named Lee and myself. The Master Sergeant said, in a mellow tone, *"Come on, boys."* I looked at Lee and he at me: *Not to worry, pal. My dad spoke with Il Capo Di Tutti Capi last night.*

As I went through the various parts of the physical examination, I met a lot of different military personnel. They were all spit-shined and highly polished individuals with crew cuts. I, on the other hand, was a hippie. I had long, curly hair that fell about my shoulders like a lion's mane. Most of the Army guys were civil to me but one guy, a Private who looked about my age, went out of his way to be rude to me. He made offensive remarks about my hair, calling me unpatriotic for growing it that long. I ignored him. But as I turned a corner on my way to yet another test, this Private and I met head on. I tried to step out of his way but he purposely knocked my packet of paperwork on the floor, scattering the contents all over the place. Then he pushed me, nearly sending me flying head over heels. Before I could react, a Lieutenant, who seemed to materialize out of thin air, stepped forward and roared, *"Private!!! Pick up this man's papers, apologize to him and report to my office. NOW!!!"* The Private did all he was ordered and left. The Lieutenant, a black man with a chiseled chin and a muscular build that seemed carved out of granite, said to me, "There was no need for that. He should know better." I said, "Thank you, Sir." The Lieutenant asked if I was in school and I told him I was about to graduate with a Bachelor of Science degree. "Are you a scientist?" he asked. "Nope," I said. "I'm a bass player." He laughed because he was a bass player too. We compared notes and found that we liked the same music and shared a lot of the same influences. He said he enjoyed meeting me and that he'd see me later. Then, he was on his way.

The final part of the physical examination was the blood pressure test. When it came my turn, I sat in a chair and rested my left arm on a small table. The doctor put the cuff around my upper arm and squeezed a little bulb that was at the end of a tube connected to the cuff. When the cuff was inflated with air, he opened a value and the cuff deflated. As the doctor read the gauge, his facial expression became one of concern. *"Son,"* he said, *"Your heart is about to burst. Your pressure is 170/110."* I didn't know what that meant. The doctor said he'd have to call his superior officer. He made a phone call and a minute later his boss walked in the room. I turn to see my friend, the Lieutenant, smiling at me. "Long time no see," he said. The doctor asked us if we knew each other. The Lieutenant said that we were old friends. The doctor explained to the Lieutenant that I had a very high blood pressure reading. A look of concern comes over the Lieutenant's face, as it had the doctor's. The Lieutenant wrote a note at the bottom of one of the pages in my packet and signed his name to it. The Lieutenant then instructed me to stop by his office before I go to lunch. *"Lunch?"* I thought to myself. I'd forgotten that I hadn't eaten all day. The Lieutenant gave me a meal ticket that entitled me to a free lunch at the restaurant across the street. I thanked him, promised to meet him in his office in one hour and went across the street to feast, courtesy of the US Army. The meal ticket used the term "One Free Lunch" but I didn't know what that meant. How much food equaled a free lunch? So I asked at the counter and the man said a free lunch equaled as much as I could fit on my tray. Well, I had a fair knowledge of physics, trigonometry, geometry, probabilities and statistics and I used every formula I could recall in order to maximize my space potential and optimize my usage of said space. The result was a wonderful mélange of lasagna, meatloaf, mashed potatoes with gravy, corn, a half loaf of Italian bread with butter, six chocolate chip cookies and a glass of Coca-Cola. There was a part of me that thought, *"Perhaps the Army is not so bad after all."*

I met the Lieutenant in his office precisely one hour later and he invited me to sit down. "I'm going to tell you something now," he said. "Listen to me closely, do as I say and everything will be fine." I listened. The Lieutenant said that my blood pressure was so high that I stood a good chance of being deferred from military service. But I had to follow his instructions to the letter. He said that the Army would call me back the following Monday, Tuesday and Wednesday to check my pressure again. They need to get three high readings. If it is high three readings in a row, I'd get a six-week deferment. But you must demand a six-month deferment, the Lieutenant said. The fellow in charge of such procedures, a Colonel, was not a nice man, according to the Lieutenant, and I believed him. He had been straight with me so far and I trusted him. The Lieutenant told me that, assuming my pressure is high on Tuesday, I must refuse to submit to another test on Wednesday. By law, the original pressure reading counts as one of the three. The Lieutenant said that the Colonel would go through the roof when I refused to come back on Wednesday, but I was to stand strong. I said I understood. The Lieutenant said to go back to Room 54 and wait for the Master Sergeant to give me a card with my instructions on it. This I did. The Lieutenant said that I must meet him in his office Monday morning at 7AM and he'd go with me to the blood pressure reading. I thanked him, shook his hand and walked down the hall to Room 54.

"Gentlemen," said the Master Sergeant in his booming voice, *"all but two of you will be in This Man's Army in three weeks."* Everyone gulped but I knew I was one of the two who would not be inducted into *That Man's Ar*my in three weeks. The Master Sergeant called the name of my buddy, Lee. He stood and walked to the front of the room. Lee was handed an index card that he did not read. He just took it from the Master Sergeant's hand and headed for the door. Then the Master Sergeant called my name. Another friend of mine, who had a super-sized file folder in a leather carrying case, was sure that his name would be called. He felt his file folder would do the trick but it didn't. So when my name was called, he lunged across the two desks between us and grabbed me by the throat. He was trying to strangle me. He was screaming obscenities at me. The Master Sergeant was down the aisle as fast as lightning and pulled my friend off me as if he were a ragdoll. The Master Sergeant was one strong guy. *"God damned fool,"* he yelled at my friend, who was by now in tears. He fell apart. But the Army took him anyway and off he was shipped to Viet Nam. I'm happy to report that he came home safe and sound after his tour of duty. The Master Sergeant

handed me my index card and I was out the door. It was weird, as I have said, because I know I could have thrived in the Army if not for the fact that I surely would have died in Viet Nam. I was (and am) as clumsy as any who walk God's green Earth. I had gotten to know a number of Army guys in the five or six hours I was at Whitehall Street and except for a couple, they were good folks.

I was back at the Lieutenant's office on Monday at 7AM. He greeted me with a warm hello and walked with me to the doctor's room. They put the blood pressure cuff on my left upper arm and squeezed the bulb. My pressure was high. Anything above 140/90 was considered too high. The doctor marked my blood pressure reading on the index card that the Master Sergeant gave me the week before and signed it. The Lieutenant then said to follow him. The next stop was the Colonel's office. The Lieutenant handed him my index card and pointed out that my pressure was high. The Colonel signed it and said, "See you tomorrow, son." That was Monday. I was back in the Lieutenant's office at 7AM the next day, Tuesday, and we went through the drill same as the day before. Again, my pressure was too high. Again, the Lieutenant walked me to the Colonel's office but this time we stopped a few paces before reaching the door. "OK, Ventura," said the Lieutenant. "Now you have to be a man. No matter what the Colonel says to you, stand strong and tell him that you know your rights. Tell him that you respectfully invoke rule number such and such in the military code. Tell him that you have failed three blood pressure exams in a row including your first physical. Tell him you refuse to return tomorrow for another blood pressure exam and demand a six-month deferment." The Lieutenant continued, "He's going to blow his top but stand strong and do what I say." A thought struck me at that moment: "Why is the Lieutenant being so nice to me? Why is he treating me so good and showing me ways to be legally deferred from military service?" I wondered but I sure as hell did not ask him. I just did as he said. The Colonel signed my index card and said, "See you tomorrow, son." But this time I repeated verbatim what the Lieutenant instructed me to say. The Colonel slammed his hands palms down on his desk. It sounded like a bomb exploded. He then fired abuses and obscenities at me as if they were being shot from a machine gun. I thought I was going to wet my pants but I stood there, expressionless, unflinching. I knew that my life depended on it, literally. If I blinked, the next stop would be Viet Nam. Perhaps frustrated by my resolve, the Colonel signed my index card. I thanked him. He said nothing and looked down at some papers on the desk. I left the room. The Lieutenant was waiting outside. He had heard everything. He smiled and shook my hand heartily, "*Well done*." Phase 1 is complete, now for Phase 2.

I was overjoyed when I received a six-month deferment in the mail a few days later. I continued to visit the Lieutenant regularly however. We were becoming friends. I was in the halls of Whitehall Street so often the army guys thought I joined up. One day, the Lieutenant said that I would be receiving another draft notice from the Selective Service. I would be instructed to report for another round of blood pressure tests. He said that this time, if my pressure was too high, I must insist on a 4F: unfit for military service on the basis of chronic high blood pressure. The Lieutenant said that the Army would keep testing my pressure until it went down to normal. At that point I would be inducted into the service. The concept behind this practice was that the inductee would eventually lose the anxiety that caused the blood pressure to spike. But the law governing such matters actually stated that, after the initial three tests, the individual is only to be tested once. Again, I was to repeat the same process as I did six months earlier. Again, I would be subject to the wrath of the Colonel. Again, I must stand strong. I followed the Lieutenant's orders. It was the same scene as the last time. He smacked his desk with the palms of his hands, cussed and spewed forth his thoughts regarding my long hair and the sorry state the country would be in if left in the hands of sad specimens such as myself. I did not flinch, although he made a good point. Lots of guys were going to Viet Nam to do their service for the U.S. Nobody wanted to be there but they went because they answered the call. Hell, several friends of mine were in Viet Nam at that very moment, guys with whom I went through my first physical six months earlier. Still, I said nothing and stood emotionless, poker-faced, determined. The Colonel uttered a disgusted sigh, signed my index card and slid it across the desk to me. He said nothing more. I did not thank him but picked up the index card and left. With the stroke of his pen, the Colonel had given me back my life. The Lieutenant and I went out for breakfast afterwards. I treated.

I received my 4F card in the mail a week later. I stopped by the Lieutenant's office and thanked him again. We walked across the street for a cup of coffee and sat quietly at a corner table. I could not deny myself the opportunity to ask the Lieutenant why he had been so kind to me. He took a sip of coffee, looked out the window to the street. He was suddenly a million miles away. After a few seconds, he turned to me and said, "I gotta go." He finished his coffee, smiled, shook my hand and left. I sat there for a few minutes, alone, and contemplated the events of the past six months. What a strange trip. Now I saw myself standing on the centerline of a deserted highway in the middle of nowhere. The road ahead became a pinpoint on the horizon. Between that pinpoint on the horizon and me was my life. I finished my coffee and started walking.

Dad's Boots

1977 was a thin year for me, financially. I was trying to break into the music business as a studio musician and it was slow going. Month after month I'd have to sell one of my basses to pay the rent. It was difficult. My first wife had just left me and I had not yet met my second wife (to whom I am still married).

Once again, second thoughts plagued me. This was a hard life, playing music for a living in America. No one gives a rat's ass about music here. It would be much more lucrative to follow in my father's footsteps and kill people for a living. I really did not have a problem shooting some stranger in the back of the head. I basically hated people anyway. I was nice to people because I thought it was the right thing to do. But it was not easy always turning the other cheek, saying "No problem!" and smiling at people who sneered at me. I'd much rather slit their throats. However, I really liked to play my bass and I liked hanging out with the studio musicians with whom I was quickly becoming close friends. I loved the funky music we'd play and I loved the fact that I could communicate with other human beings via music, not words, and not violence.

Late one night in February 1977 I drove my beat up old Honda Civic down to a really cool music club called *Michael's.* This was where all the studio musicians gathered to jam and have a good time. There was a band of these musicians who called themselves *The New York Music Mob* (oddly enough). This band epitomized the music scene in New York City in the late 1970's. They would play individually and collectively on recording sessions each day for all the top recording and singing stars, making thousands of dollars each week. At night, they would come together to play for themselves and their friends, hosting jam sessions and eventually developing a repertoire that included funky versions of Gershwin's "Rhapsody In Blue." It was freezing cold on this particular winter evening. It had snowed and I did not have the proper boots for such weather. Further, I did not have the $5.00 door charge to gain entrance into *Michael's.* However, *Michael's* had a big, plexiglass side window through which one could look at the bandstand and through which one could hear the band. I had spent many a night at this window the previous summer. The New York heat and humidity that plagued people during the daytime had cooled out by 2AM. The funky rhythms, mixtures of reggae, Motown, the sound of Philadelphia, blues and jazz, mixed together in a sublimely infectious beat that caused everyone, including those on the sidewalk, to dance. It was quite a different story in the winter. The beats were still funky as dog shit, but the feet were too cold to dance. I wore red Converse All-stars, the only pair of shoes that I owned. When I played at weddings, my dad would lend me a real nice suit and a beautiful pair of Italian leather boots.

One day Dad called me up and said, "Come to the house, I have a present for you." I ran over and he presented me with his Italian leather boots. He knew I loved them. They were brand new. I don't think he ever wore them. I cherished those boots and I still have them. They are still the coolest boots on earth.

But on this particular night, I was wearing the red Cons and my toes were frozen. From the corner of my eye I saw someone looking at me a few feet away. I turned to see the great gospel pianist (and member of *The New York Music Mob)* Richard T. Funk looking at me in amazement. He had stepped outside for a cigarette. "What are you doing standing in the freezing cold at 2AM?" he asked. I explained that I often come to *Michael's* to hear *The New York Music Mob* but that I never have any money to pay the door charge. So I listen from the sidewalk. He smiled a big smile, one that I would see many more times in the years to come and said, "Come with me." Richard led me through the kitchen, into the club and sat me down at the band's table. Richard flagged down a waitress and said:

"Please get my friend anything he wants and put it on my tab."

He didn't even know my name. But somehow we had an instant connection.

The waitress asked me, "What'll it be?" I immediately answered, "Coca-Cola and large French fries."

Meantime, Richard sat at the piano and began a solo version of Gershwin's *Rhapsody In Blue*. As he slowly began to swing it, one by one the entire band joined the jamming. The set lasted, non-stop, for two hours. I was in funky heaven. Afterwards, Richard joined me at the table and we talked for an hour. I told him I was a bass player in a Top 40 band but I would love to break into record dates. He invited me to a jam session that they were having the next evening. I jumped at the opportunity. 24 hours after meeting Richard, I was playing bass in a jam session with the very same guys I stood in the snow to see the previous evening. Richard liked my bass playing and soon began recommending me to various producers. I began to get calls for record dates (recording sessions). I was actually earning a living, albeit a meager one, as a studio and touring musician in New York City.

It was during this time that I met a recording engineer who helped me get work as a record producer. Producers are the ones who direct the recording sessions, who basically see to it that the music gets recorded in time, on time, in tune, on budget and in as an efficient and effective manner as possible. Producers are therapists to temperamental artists, liaisons to record companies and commander-in-chiefs of recording sessions. I found that I enjoyed this new role, this new challenge, although it was far more stressful than simply playing my bass and going home (not that playing a musical instrument on a record date is simple). I widened my circle of friends, moved out of the City and into a beautiful home in Westchester County and worked every night, all night. The music industry, at least the creative side of it, runs on the other end of the clock. Day is night and night is day. I worked from sundown to sunup for 20 years. I realized more of my dreams than I even dreamt. I worked mostly for independent record labels, those that are not associated with the major, global conglomerates. I was not comfortable around the phony baloney jerk-offs who shook your hand and stabbed you in the back at the same time. I found that the smaller record labels were run by people who cared about the music first and foremost. The globalization of music product distribution via the internet had not yet arrived. One needed a network of distributors in regions nationwide in order to place product in stores. Music was still purchased over the counter, not online and certainly not as digital downloads yet. Essentially, I followed the times and trends, the dot com revolution and watched the music industry morph into its present, artist-friendly state. One can build a viable musical career for herself/himself with no assistance whatever from a major corporation. The hold that these global super-corporations once had on artists has been broken by technology. Artists who aspire to have superstar careers must partner with major labels. However the real-deal artists who live and suffer for their music can make a little bit of money, make ends meet, and live free from the meddling and deceit of the corporate scumbags. It's the legal and bloodless way to slit the throats of the motherfuckers that my dad, Sammy and Patsy would have slaughtered (in the literal sense of the word) back in the day.

Although these were stressful, difficult times, I found a great satisfaction in knowing that I was earning my living as a producer and musician. A friend of mine, who himself was trying to follow the same path as me (i.e. earn a living in music on his own terms rather than join the "family business" and *certainly* not give up his independence and sense of pride working for a big corporation) gave me words of wisdom that I have never forgotten and with which I wholeheartedly agree:

I'd rather eat the grass in the park and sleep under a tree than eat caviar and sleep at a four-star hotel if it meant working for those corporate bastards.

Jackie The Ripper

It was a struggle finding work as a producer in the early days of my music career. In the late 70s and early 80s, I was still part mobster and part musician. I was trying to become established as a record producer. This was much more difficult than gigging as a bass player in disco bands. I had plenty of those gigs. I was still doing them. It was a different story getting people to entrust their music and money to a producer who had no track record. But how does one establish a track record if no one will trust him? Well, I have never been one to fuck around with people. I would go to clubs, listen to artists perform, and if I liked what I heard, offer them money to sign production deals with me. I had a partner named Jackie "The Ripper" Anthony. We called him "The Ripper" because his weapon of choice was one of those tri-pronged claw things that you use to dig in your garden. Only Jackie The Ripper sharpened those prongs to where they were like ice picks. He'd go right for your eyes. Jackie could tear half your face off with one swipe of that thing. He had several of them, all with rubber grips and highest quality steel tips. I have seen Jackie The Ripper take a guy's eyes out with one swipe, as quick as a cat. It was amazing. Pending the Ripper's mission, he would either let the guy suffer for a while and then, with a mighty swing, rip the guy's throat out, killing him instantly or, if he was in a tranquil mood, he would say to the guy he just blinded, "I'll let it go this time, but watch it in the future. I'll send the doc over to patch you up." Craziest bird I ever met.

Jackie funded all of my music projects. There were any number of disco divas trying to make it in the music business and for us it was like shooting fish in a barrel. Jackie didn't know anything about producing records and never interfered with my studio decisions. His thing was publicity and marketing. Jackie owned a number of discos and he would feature our artists in the clubs. He was very courteous to the artists. We treated them like queens. We didn't sign male artists unless they were part of the bands we signed. Jackie would wine and dine these girls but never tried to bed them. He had plenty of girlfriends. We were trying very seriously to make a viable record label. We put out a number of 12-inch 45 RPM singles but none of them made any noise. Even with the ability to put the girls on stage, we couldn't attract the attention of the major labels for distribution. Although I detested the thought of dealing with major labels, we needed their help. We had taken things as far as we could on our own.

Ultimately, the girls would get bummed and ask to be released from their contracts. Even then, Jackie was considerate. He would let them go most of the time. It was only when he felt we hadn't yet done all we could do that Jackie would ask them to give us more time. They usually gave us another shot. After all, we were flush with cash. Jackie drove a big Cadillac, dressed impeccably, and was a sweet guy even when he was pissed. There were times that we did not agree on a particular issue and he would always say to me:

"Trouble, you're a stubborn bastard and you drive me fucking crazy sometimes. But I love you."

I have found that throughout my life, I have been perfectly comfortable around real-deal tough guys. It didn't matter to me that they were murderers. I loved them and they loved me. We all belonged to the same union, *International Brotherhood of Murderers, Thugs & Thieves*.

Anyway, one of our artists wanted out of her contract. Jackie didn't really want to let her go because we had booked her for a bunch of club appearances up and down the East Coast. Jackie was super connected. But she was not having it, no matter how much he pleaded with her. Yes, Jackie The Ripper got on one knee, like he was proposing, and begged her to stay. We had a shitload of money invested in her and she was finally starting to get a little notice in the press and trade papers. Her latest single was starting to appear on club charts and even on some radio charts. It was just bad timing. We really needed her to stay and cooperate. But she said she was going to sue us if we didn't release her from her contract. Now one thing you didn't do was give Jackie The Ripper an ultimatum. We looked into the matter and found out that an attorney who had connections to a major label had won our little diva away from us with promises of major stardom overnight. So we stopped by his office on Madison Avenue in New York City. We were dressed in our finest suits, we smelled good, we looked sharp and we were sharp. Our intentions were honorable. We just wanted to have a discussion, explain to the man that we had a lot of money wrapped up in her, and he was putting ideas in her head.

Jackie said: *"Would you work with us on this project? We would pay you handsomely."*

Instead of answering us civilly, like a gentleman, and perhaps considering our offer, the lawyer said:

"Why the fuck would I want to get involved with a couple of two-bit mobsters like you stupid fucks?"

Jackie said, *"Thank you for your time."*

I thought to myself, *"Goodbye to you, Mr. Lawyer."*

We left the office and waited in Jackie's Caddy across the street. We watched every single person who left the building, we drank coffee, we ate a couple slices of pizza, and we kept waiting. Jackie had a special tag that hung from his rear view mirror. It had some kind of official NYC insignia on it. All I know is that we were parked in a *No Parking* zone for five hours and no one bothered us. Jackie The Ripper was super connected. Around 9PM, Mr. Lawyer left the building and we followed on foot, far behind. We kept weaving in and out of the zillion pedestrians on the street, always keeping the scumbag in sight. Soon Mr. Lawyer entered a highbrow jetset bar with us on his ass. He hoisted a few with some pals. The place was crowded and we blended into the mass of people. We watched and waited as Mr. Lawyer kept banging back the Scotches. After about an hour he paid his tab and staggered out the door en route to Penn Station and the Long Island Railroad. We followed in the shadows and as soon as he passed a dark alley, which were plentiful in the cross streets he would inevitably have to take in order to get to Penn Station, we pounced on him. He didn't know what hit him.

He was half drunk and we came out from behind a parked car. Jackie hit him high and I hit him low. We dragged him deep into the bowels of the alley and we beat the shit out of him. Mr. Lawyer was stunned. He didn't know what was happening. We gave him a few minutes to compose himself and he sure as hell sobered up quickly. He recognized us:

"Guys," he said, *"please forgive my indiscretion this afternoon. We can work this out. I've been thinking about it and I'd LOVE to be your attorney. No Charge."*

The guy was bleeding from his mouth, his eye, his nose, which was broken, and he was shaking like a leaf.

"What do you say, Mr. Anthony?" I asked Jackie.

"I don't know, Mr. Ventura," he answered.

"Well, Mr. Anthony," I reply, *"perhaps we would do well to give this gentleman the benefit of the doubt? He seems sincere."*

"Quite so, Mr. Ventura," responded Jackie. *"Perhaps it would be a wise decision to consider his offer."*

Jackie and I stroked our chins, feigned deep thought, and smiled.

"Yes!" shouts Jackie. *"Yes, sir, we accept your offer!"*

Mr. Lawyer breathes a deep sigh of relief. Then Jackie reaches out and grabs my arm:

"Hold on a moment, Mr. Ventura."

"What is it, Mr. Anthony?" I inquired.

"Didn't this gentleman call us - what was it – 'two-bit mobsters', Mr. Ventura?" asks Jackie.

"By Jove, I believe you're right, sir," I returned.

"This rather muddies the water, does it not, Mr. Anthony?"

The poor bastard is shitting his pants now. Even he knows it's over. Jackie looks at the fuck-head and says, civilized as you please:

"We are sorry, sir, but we must decline your kind offer."

Jackie pulls out his three-pronged implement of destruction and the guy tries to scream, "NO!" But before he could even take a breath, Jackie ripped the lawyer's face off. He hit him time and again until the front of the guy's skull was exposed. His eyes were gone, his nose was gone and Jackie even knocked the guy's teeth down his throat. Then he scalped the piece of shit. He raked that fucking claw over the guy's head time and again until the top of his skull was exposed too. When the esteemed attorney was suitably mangled and definitely dead, we cleaned ourselves off with our monogrammed handkerchiefs and walked calmly back to the Cadillac, which still sat unmolested in a *No Parking* zone.

Jackie said, *"I'm hungry, you hungry?"*

"I'm always hungry," I said.

So we went back to the bar that Mr. Lawyer had just left and we ordered steaks (this is before I became vegetarian). The diva that started this thing came back to us, only now it was her turn to beg. Jackie said:

"What about your new attorney? I thought he was going to hook you up?"

She said, *"I changed my mind. I decided that I REALLY want to stay with you. I love you guys. I could never leave you."*

Jackie The Ripper looks at her and said, *"No, no. We wouldn't hear of it. You go with him. Here is your release."*

Jackie hands her a piece of paper releasing her from her obligations. She took it with a trembling hand. Jackie gave her a look as cold as ice and then turned away.

We continued our recording endeavors for another year or so, always hoping for that hit record. No other artists asked to be released from their deals. But one day Jackie called me up and asked to get together. We met at our usual spot, Aunt Angie's Diner. Jackie looked scared, which puzzled me. Nothing scared him. He said:

"Trouble, I got cancer."

"What the fuck, Jackie?" I say.

"I didn't tell you but I've been puking blood for a few months," he said. *"I saw the doc. I got about a month."*

"Oh, Jackie, no," I say, my own voice trembling now.

He reached across the table, took my hand: *"I'm scared, Trouble."*

I said, *"Fuck that doctor. I'll stay with you, we'll beat this thing."*

I tried, I really did. I brought him to holistic doctors and faith healers and other medical doctors. But six weeks after our meeting at Aunt Angie's, Jackie The Ripper died in the hospital as I held his hand. His last words were: *"May all your dreams come true, Trouble."*

Without my partner, I wasn't in the mood to run the label and I just didn't have Jackie's nerve when it came to the art of persuasion. So I went back to hustling live gigs and record dates. I sent out resumes, and the few semi-hits that Jackie and I had produced actually attracted the attention of creative directors at a number of independent labels. Before too long, I was hired as a staff producer by one of these labels. From there, other job offers followed and I have not been out of work since. I owe my success to a lot of people: my dad, Fat Patsy, Richard T. Funk and others, not the least of which was an absolutely insane motherfucker who slaughtered people with a tri-pronged garden tool, but who believed in me and in no small way put me on the map, Jackie "The Ripper" Anthony.

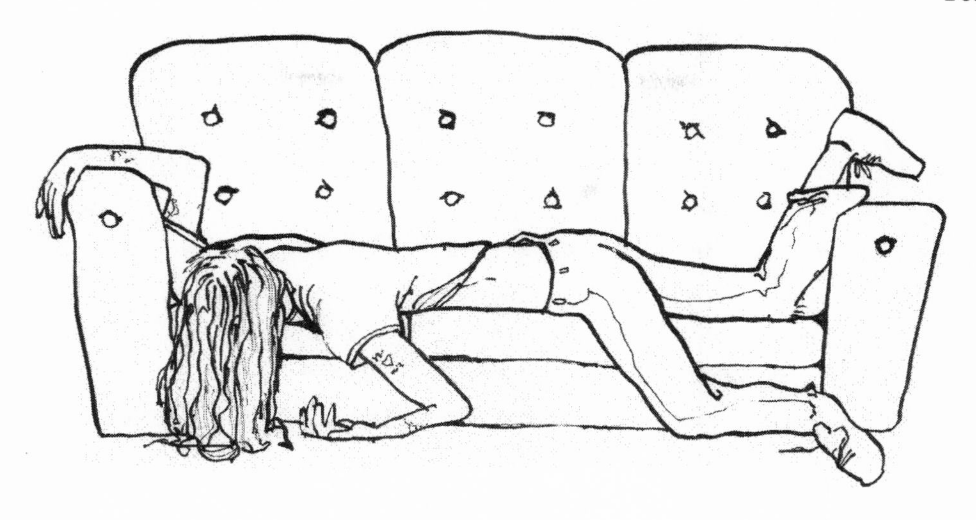

Psychopaths In The Studio

I used to lie in bed at night and pray to God, *"Please let me make my living in the recording studios."* It was all I wanted to do once I got a taste of that world. I had worked with the studio jam band *The New York Music Mob* and I had begun to get calls as a bassist and as a producer. Most of the people I produced in the late 70s and early 80s were signed to my own record label. My partner, Jackie The Ripper, had recently died of stomach cancer and I was giving it all I had, trying to network and become an in-demand session bassist and producer. Things were starting to click a bit and as time went on I began to work so much that in the course of a 10-year period I had perhaps a month off, a day here and there. But you have to be careful what you wish for. I got to work with many of my idols, real deal artists, people who changed the course of music. I made real records not "pop" records. The only thing was the artists with whom I worked were completely psychotic. I was used to being around nuts. My dad and the guys in the crew were not wrapped very tightly. But it was cool for them to be eccentric. They killed people for a living. You don't expect those kinds of guys to be Sunday school teachers. But the artists with whom I worked were music masters. They had the power to move people with music. They were magicians as far as I was concerned. I could understand a hired killer being a bit cranky every now and then. That particular occupation is stressful. Sometimes they even had trouble sleeping, although not often. The mob guys didn't make people jump for joy when they went to work. They made people die. These artists made people jump and sing and dance when they went to work. They made people happy. I could not understand such pains-in-the-ass being so depressed all the time. Agreed, their drug and alcohol habits and such were not conducive to happiness as a rule, but when they picked up their instruments and began to play, I felt like I could fly. I learned to be a real musician just by being around these people, by working with them, by speaking with them and by watching them. What the fuck did they have to be so unhappy about? Life deals everyone shit on a shingle from time to time. The Lord never said that life would be an easy walk. Life is difficult. I know that. But I was getting older now and I was seeing the awesome power these folks possessed.

I could not understand why they were always depressed, angry and worst of all, abusive to me. One motherfucker actually slapped my hand during a playback because I was whispering an instruction to the engineer and he wanted it silent. Now, I don't need to tell you that if Jackie were still my partner, the world would be minus one rock star. I just let it go because the goal was to get the track. I practically had to wipe their asses. Another time I was working with a guy who was so stressed out he was hollering at everyone in sight. I was on the phone with the guy's record label when he exploded out of the studio and into the office:

SHUT THE FUCK UP! I'M TRYING TO LISTEN TO THE PLAYBACK IN THE STUDIO!

Of course, I had to eat shit again and say, "So sorry. I'll keep it down." But I really don't think I was speaking loud enough to be heard in the next room. I was thinking, "If only Jackie were here!" He would not have taken the approach that I took.

Jackie would have said, *"Too noisy in here for you, pal? No problem! I'll just shove your fucking head up your ass. That ought to muffle the sound, no?"* Jackie had a different methodology than I did.

Drugs, as I have noted, played a big role in these artists' daily lives and routines. They would go from happy to angry the moment the weed was finished or the last beer was drunk. We had a network of drug dealers to keep the supply constant. I really didn't care if they overdosed and died. I didn't see that as my problem. In that sense, the mob mentality never left me. *Fuck them*. If they wanted to dose themselves into oblivion, that was their prerogative. I just needed to get my records made. Sometimes the dealers would come to the studio to watch the sessions. They were a distraction but a necessary one. If the artists saw the dealers actually in the studio, they knew their drug stream would not dry up. In particular, there was a dealer who cut a very scary appearance. He lost an eye in a knife fight. He was actually a nice guy but since he didn't wear a patch over the eye in question, it was pretty intimidating to see. We called him *"Uno"*. He liked me because I gave him a corn muffin. Go figure. Sometimes my dad and a few of the guys would visit. They would bring enough food to feed a third world country. Everybody ate and drank so much that it pretty much ended the session. The crew brought up veal cutlet parmesan sandwiches. One of the musicians, a stoner from the 60s, asked what veal was.

Fat Patsy said, *"Veal is the meat of a baby cow, a calf."*

"No shit?" said the stoner. *"I thought veal was a vegetable."*

I didn't know whether Patsy was going to laugh or throw the stoner out the window. He had one of those looks on his face. It could have gone either way. Then they light up a spliff and smoked themselves into orbit. The mob guys loved to smoke weed with my hippie and musician friends.

A *very famous* producer with a raging drug habit once visited me in the studio. Although he was a good friend of mine, I was not expecting him to drop by and, frankly, I was not happy when he did. He was a wacko, extremely disruptive and rude. I happened to be working with a world-renowned blues singer. My maniac friend was so cranked on cocaine that he was literally climbing the walls, or at least the molding that rimmed the studio walls.

My wacko famous producer friend was screaming: *"Sing it, man. Put your ass into it."*

The artist, a regal gentleman, was looking at him with a combination of anger, confusion and disdain. This was not a good thing. I had to have my pal escorted from the studio. He didn't mind. He was used to being thrown out of most everywhere he went. I felt bad. I was able to get the session back on track and a wonderful single resulted. But my buddy drifted off into space and I have lost contact with him. I hope he is retired and happy, living on a farm somewhere. But more likely, he is drifting aimlessly about the globe, crashing at some star's home until he or she is tired of his nonsense. Then it's back to the street.

One guy died on the couch in the studio. He was shooting heroin and he overdosed. Again, my mob attitude kicked in. Everyone was running around shouting:

"Call an ambulance! Get the police!"

I was bummed that the session would have to be cancelled. A rock press writer asked me to comment on the tragic event. My comment was:

"The fucking asshole cost me ten grand today by dying."

Taken aback, the writer asked: *"Doesn't his passing make you sad?"*

I continued: *"The only thing I'm sad about is all the money the loser cost me by dying on my couch."*

I was actually angry with this wonderfully talented individual for wasting his life and his art on drugs. In truth, his death left me heartbroken. But I had a hard time expressing myself in those days. I was happy or sad, docile or agitated, calm or enraged. There was no middle ground. I was not reasonable. So such stupid remarks were common.

I have come to learn that people are people, no matter their occupation or avocation. They are all, basically, ball-breakers. They are spoiled brats who spit in the face of The Lord because they do not appreciate the rare and God-given gift of success that has been bestowed upon them. That is something I will never understand. I have shoveled shit against the tide, as my dad would say, to become successful as a musician, producer and college educator. I have met a succession of pompous assholes at every turn of the road in my life. The term "asshole" was coined for these pompous fucks, I think. Somebody said:

"Hey, let's come up with a name to describe someone with unrealistically high self-esteem."

"Goose"

No! That is only a small part of it.

"Gas Bag?"

No. It needs to say more.

"Dick?"

Closer.

Rat Bastard?

It's almost there. We need to combine all of the above.

"Asshole!"

THAT'S IT!

You can include assholes from the entertainment, sports, political and academic industries in there, to name but a few.

Another interesting thing about record production is the inordinate amount of bullshit that one hears. Wannabe numb nuts who have no careers and no hope of ever having careers are the first to say:

This is one of Jimi Hendrix's Strats.

I jammed with The Doors.

I jammed with Stevie Wonder.

I was a close friend of Jim Morrison's.

I was a close friend of Janis Joplin's.

I was a close friend of ________________________________ (fill in the blank with the name of any dead rock star).

The place was packed.

The A&R guy from SONY Records was at the gig.

We're getting signed by SONY Records.

I wrote "Celebration".

They loved us.

I invented 4-on-the-floor.

I partied with the Grateful Dead.

By the beginning of the new millennium, I started to become very anxious and out of sorts. It was a weird feeling. These people, all artists whom I dreamed of working with, were miserable, ungrateful and spoiled. Worse, they were making other people, especially me, unhappy. It was horrible. I wasn't at the crossroads yet, but I could see it approaching on the horizon. I thought: *"Perhaps teaching full-time is the answer."*

The world is full of scumbags. I was about to meet a highly educated brand of scumbag and a thoroughly uneducated brand of scumbag. The only things that they had in common were:

1. Most of them had never done anything on a professional level and

2. Most of them thought that the most important day in history was their birthdays.

I was heading straight into a nest of hornets.

Tom-Tom's

Thomas "Tom-Tom" Tomassino owned a couple of nightclubs in the City. When Jackie The Ripper died of cancer, his family sold his clubs to various guys in that end of the business. Tom-Tom bought two. One of them was in the Bronx and the other one in Yonkers. Tom-Tom's was the one in the Bronx. It was truly a hole in the wall. Patrons walked in the front door to be faced by a plexiglass wall. There were doorways on either side. The right side led you to the bar, the left to the restaurant. A four-foot high partition separated the two areas. The bandstand was in the back on the left and the kitchen and bathrooms were in the back on the right. The entire place was as big as a Dunkin' Donuts, only the food wasn't as good. Tom-Tom's was a hangout for mob guys, especially drug dealers. It was the early 80's and cocaine was still the drug of choice with the low-life set as well as the jetset. The freaks who frequented Tom-Tom's were members of the former set. The guys were slime balls and the women were *puttanas*.

My band played at all the nightclubs in the City and we were at Tom-Tom's for weeks at a time. It was great fun. We made real good money and ate and drank for free. We were very popular, which was great for the ego. The girls were always flirting with us and offering us drugs and sex. Apart from the fact that I was married to my current wife by this time, I was not interested in catching crabs and whatever other creepy crawly bugs were flourishing between their legs. The guys were pieces of work. Wannabe racketeers who thought they were Al Capone reincarnated. They walked with a swagger, bragged that they were killer hit men (a sure sign that they were not) and said *"How ya doin'?"* to everybody. They were absolute morons, dumb as rocks, and complete losers. They dressed nice, though.

I was trying to stay out of the mob stuff at this point and steered clear of most of the characters that hung at Tom-Tom's. But you could always tell when, on the rare occasion, a real mob guy came in. He was usually older, sometimes in his seventies or even eighties. He had a bevy of stunningly beautiful women with him and he arrived late, after midnight. On such occasions, I knew we'd be making some serious money. *The Don* would always ask us to keep playing after hours. We just kept going until dawn. *The Don* would finally look at his watch and say to his entourage, *"Andiamo"* (Italian for "Let's go"). He would walk up to the bandstand, shake my hand, and say:

"Magnifico, Trouble. Salute! A presto."

He would then hand me a wad of cash that could choke a horse. It was usually $500, which effectively doubled our pay for the night.

I had a friend of sorts named Screwy Louie. Louie was a bonafide psycho. He was addicted to cocaine and did whatever it took to keep his habit satisfied. He was a big guy and had no problem collecting the vig on loans for the loan sharks. He was great at beating the shit out of the petrified dopes who found themselves in arrears of loan sharks. Most of them forked over everything they had in their pockets at the sight of Louie. If he were in a good mood, if the money was sufficient, and if this was his first visit, he'd let them off with a warning. If not, no one could deter Louie from his mission. Louie never killed anyone. That would defeat the purpose. His job was to collect money. His methodology, as described above, would invariably leave the target of his mission a bloody pulp of shredded flesh and broken bones. Louie was a nut job, but I liked him. He was a Neanderthal, yes, but he had a good heart. He saw his "profession" as strictly business, nothing personal. He was very generous, possessed a quick wit and was very soft spoken. Louie was a gentleman when in the company of my wife and I trusted him to be alone with her. He would often come to our house for dinner. He even took my wife to the mall shopping. He loved to shop. Considering what he did for a living, I found this rather odd. But as I said, he was a unique character. One night my band was playing at Tom-Tom's and it happened to be my birthday. I was in the bathroom on a break, standing at the urinal. I was concentrating on the business at hand when an arm reached from behind me, above my right shoulder. Attached to the arm was a tattooed hand that I immediately recognized as Louie's. The tattooed hand held a switchblade, opened. On the blade was a line of cocaine.

"Happy Birthday, Trouble," said Louie.

"I can't, Louie. Thanks, anyway," I said.

I explained to him that my doctors were concerned with my health, especially my heart. I had chronic high blood pressure.

"Oh, man, I'm so sorry," said Louie.

He bought me a fine black silk shirt the next day. It was really nice and I wore it all the time.

Louie was arrested not long after my birthday. The charge was possession and trafficking of cocaine. I went to his trial. At the end of the hearing, Louie was asked if he had anything to say to the judge. Louie approached the Bench and said:

"Your Honor, I'm looking at 10 to 20 over here. Can I cop a plea?"

I knew that Louie had just signed his death warrant. Now, even if he kept his mouth shut, the mob boys would whack him. They couldn't trust him anymore. I don't know if Louie had received a shortened sentence but he was sent to prison then and there. I guess the next step would have been an appeal or maybe a plea bargain. But things never reached that point. Louie was killed in prison a few days later. He had been assigned to the general population and was working in the kitchen. A guard found his body slumped in a corner. Louie had been slaughtered, stabbed a few dozen times, his throat slit, his tongue severed. I wore the fine black shirt that Louie had given me for my birthday to his funeral. My dad was with me and he saw how shaken I was. Dad, in his inimitable style, said, in an effort to comfort me:

"Nobody likes a squealer, Trouble."

Louie had broken rule numero uno: *Sta Zitto! (Shut Up!)*

Lots of other odd fellows could be found at Tom-Tom's. Some were scumbags, really despicable shitheads. Others had redeeming qualities, like Screwy Louie. Another such individual was known as Artie Bots. He was given this *soprannominato* (nickname) because he was crazy. In Italian, the word for an insane person is *Pazzo (pronounced Potzo).* The slang is *"Bots."* Artie Bots was a nonviolent thief. He could steal anything from a diamond ring to an 18-wheeler. He was very intelligent, college-educated. He simply chose to be self-employed rather than work for some big corporation. He had one particularly peculiar tendency. Any time he would pass a mirror, he would stare at it for a moment and then get into an argument with himself. He'd curse at it:

"You're a fucking no-good bum."

The image in the mirror would evidently say something to Artie that he found disrespectful, although no one else could hear what Artie was hearing. In any case, Artie would be ready with a comeback.

"Oh, really? Well, fuck you too, pal. I got a college degree. You questioning my credentials?" the crazy Bots would bark back.

It got so that we didn't even notice it anymore. Sooner or later, Artie would walk away from the mirror, mumbling to himself. He was a nice guy, though. He kept telling us that he was an extra in the motion picture, *Ghostbusters.* We could never find him in the throng of people fleeing the Pillsbury Doughboy. But Bots insisted. I place this in the "arguing with mirrors" category. He swore he was a distant relative of Mussolini. He would recite historical inaccuracy after historical inaccuracy as he downed Heineken after Heineken.

On some level, Artie was an honest thief. That or he was a stupid thief. He and a cohort were each driving a stolen 18-wheeler filled with TV sets and other electronic home entertainment goods that they had hijacked. They were traveling toward New York on the Jersey Turnpike when Artie's partner in crime was pulled over by the police. It was a routine check. Instead of driving on, Bots pulled over too. So the police got two for one, courtesy of Mussolini's distant cousin. They both went to prison for a year.

Upon his release, Bots decided to go straight. He gave up his criminal activities and went to work for a bank of all places. The temptation to pick up some extra cash must have been great but he did not yield. He was true to his new life. There must not have been many mirrors in that bank because Artie caused no scenes and was, by all accounts, well-liked. A few months after starting his work at the bank, Artie Bots was in the bathroom. He came out to find a bank robbery in progress. His sudden appearance must have startled the bank robber. Before Artie knew what was happening, the bastard put a slug in his chest. Artie's was an especially sad funeral because he had tried to start a new life on the right side of the law. The police picked up the bag of shit soon after and put him in jail pending a trial that never happened. This scumbag (I never found out the bank robber's name but "scumbag" will suffice) was found absolutely slaughtered. He had killed a beloved, albeit goofy, member of our secret community at Tom-Tom's. Scumbag got the special treatment. He was dismembered while he was still alive. It must have been a gloriously painful death. They started with his fingers and worked their way up and down. He was in a total of 21 pieces when the guards found him. I take solace in the fact that he's undoubtedly rotting in hell at this moment.

The line of maniacs that were in and out of Tom-Tom's was endless. Some of them were cool and others were vile. But I found it a comfortable place to play with my band, *The Sounds Inc*. (yes, yes, an awful name). It was our home base and we spent a good part of each year there. While I was making a serious effort to further my career as a musician, I never strayed far from the comfortable bosom of life's seedy underbelly.

Even as my studio career began to blossom, I still played with my band and more often than not we could be found at Tom-Tom's.

Word

My dad and his crew had stealing down to a fine art. They hardly ever paid for anything. It was more fun to steal it. If they didn't steal it, they bought it with money they got from selling goods they had stolen. The funny thing is that Dad and his friends would GIVE you anything you wanted. They never visited anyone's house or went to a party or a dinner without bringing a week's worth of food and wine. Anytime Dad would bring us to Maryland to visit my Uncle Zoomie, he would bring steaks, ribs, whiskey, wine, vegetables, and fruit. There was enough to feed 20 people for a week. Dad was the most generous guy I ever knew. He was also one of the slickest crooks ever to walk the earth, with a temper that was explosive. Every time Dad got busted and I was with him, which was often, I ended up sitting in the waiting room of the police station while one of Dad's crew drove over to post bail and pick us up.

I was with him once when he was driving on the wrong side of the road. We were on the boulevard near the abandoned train yard. It's just one lane in each direction and we were at a standstill. My dad was not noted for his patience. He abruptly said, "Fuck this," and swerved into the opposite lane and oncoming traffic. It was like that scene in *The French Connection*. Finally, after a few blocks of swerving in and out of traffic, an unmarked police car pulled us over. The officer got out of the car and asks Dad for his license. Dad had blatant contempt for authority that he did not try to hide. Dad flips his license at the cop who dropped it on the floor. He picked up the laminated card, read the name printed on it and said:

"Now, Domenico (my dad's first name)…"

Dad said, "Don't call me by my first name, you don't know me."

The cop says, "Listen, my friend…"

Dad cut him off again: "I ain't your friend."

Now the officer is beginning to lose his patience: "Alright, pal…"

Dad cut him off again: "Go fuck your mother in hell."

That was that. On went the handcuffs and off to the police station we went. Dad did that stuff just to piss off the police. There was pretty much nothing that Dad enjoyed more. As a result, he spent quite a bit of time in lockup, waiting for his attorney to post bail.

Dad hated authority and the only thing that he hated as much was being owed money. If you owed him money he was relentless in his pursuit to retrieve it. If you stole money from him, he would come after you like a pit bull. He could steal from you but you couldn't steal from him. If he stole from you, it became his. All prior history was erased. But if you stole from him, even if you reclaimed your own money or property, he would hunt you down. If it were the first time you stole from him, he'd talk to you casually. I was with him when he visited a rather portly gent who owed him $5000 in gambling debt. It was the fellow's first offense. The guy was coughing up phlegm and blood as he said, "Breezie, I'll have the money for you on Thursday."

My dad said, "Yeah, yeah, Carmine. I don't care about the money but I worry about you. You have to take better care of yourself. Stop smoking those God damned cigarettes and lose a few pounds. I love you, Carmine."

For a minute, Dad even had me fooled. We got back into the car and Dad mumbled under his breath, "Choke to death you fat fuck." Thursday came and went and Carmine did not pay up. So Carmine's brand new Cadillac Coupe De Ville disappeared. Carmine was very lucky. If there was a second visit, it came usually with a bit of physical violence. They'd slap you around. They wouldn't cripple you but they'd put the fear of God in you (although God had nothing to do with it). The third time was the charm: you ended up in the hospital. I've seen some of the guys that needed to be visited a third time. It was horrifying. They didn't look human. They looked humanoid. Their teeth were knocked out, their skulls bashed in, their legs broken. By the time they were released from the hospital, they were more than happy to pay their tabs.

Dad lent money, booked bets, stole anything that wasn't nailed down, gambled and paid off local inspectors and union officials so that his not-quite-up-to-code construction jobs passed inspection. Next to the police, Dad hated union officials most. All of the construction jobs that Dad's companies were doing were technically supposed to be under the sanction of various construction unions. But Dad didn't like to pay union wages to the guys who worked for his companies. He paid them very well, covered them with insurance, threw them Christmas parties and gave them their birthdays off with pay. He just resented paying union dues and all the fees involved with being a union signatory. Sometimes there would be "disagreements" between Dad and the union big wigs. It would usually involve threats and a *"Fuck You"* repartee but things generally quieted down after a while. However, one time I was with him on a jobsite. Dad was talking to a union guy and I was standing in another area of the site. We were in the basement and there were open sections of the floor above us, through which the workers would pass equipment and materials. The protocol was to clear the area before sending anything up or down. I was standing beneath one of these openings when a 100-pound roll of electrical cable came crashing down beside me, missing me by inches. It would have killed me instantly. My dad came running over when he heard the crash. Once he saw I was OK, he looked up at the opening above me. He knew that someone just tried to kill me. I had seen Dad do unbelievably brutal things to people. But he just exploded. I had never seen him so angry. He was actually growling as we ran upstairs. When we got there, of course, no one was around. He bellowed at the union representative:

"One of your motherfucking pigs just tried to kill my son!"

The union rep tried to calm my dad down but that had the opposite effect. Dad walked over to the open window where there was a crew of union workers on a break. He roared at the group of snickering men:

"YOU'RE DEAD!"

Now that is a phrase that had become somewhat clichéd. Little kids used to say that to one another in my neighborhood. It didn't mean anything. But when my dad said it everyone knew he meant it, *because he never said it before this day*. That was the only time I ever heard my dad say that phrase. The snickering union scumbags knew he meant it, too. They got quiet and looked down at the ground. The union rep said, "Get back to work. Break's over." They shuffled off. My dad said to me, "Go sit in the car." I did so, while Dad went to a phone booth and made a call. Soon Dad came back to the car. He started the engine and began to sing, as he always did when driving:

Everybody loves somebody sometime…

I didn't know what was going to happen but I knew there would be payback.

The next day all the union workers and reps went busily about their business at the construction site. The guys that worked for my dad's company had been given the day off. Suddenly, the chill in the early morning air was abruptly heated as the building erupted in a geyser of flames. Everyone on the construction site was incinerated. There was nothing left of anyone but teeth and bones. The official police report said that a faulty gas line was set off by one of the workers' cigarettes. But everyone knew the truth.

No law enforcement agency, no building inspector and no union official ever spoke of the incident. No one dared. Those guys who tried to kill me yesterday were all dead today.

Dad kept his word.

Don't Fuck With Patty

My wife, Patty, is the apple of my eye. She is the apple of my father's eye as well. Dad has always thought the world of her and looked upon her as family from the moment he met her. So it goes without saying that anyone who was crazy enough to fuck with Patty had to deal with my dad. The three untouchables in my father's life were my mom, my sister and my wife. If you wronged them in *any* way, you died.

My sister brought home a few boyfriends before she married her husband, my brother-in-law Sally Boy. None of the guys she dated crossed my dad. They knew better. Anyway, they were harmless. In fact, Dad and I would watch the basketball games on TV with one of them. His name was Carlo. Dad and I called him Dollar Bill. He liked to think of himself as a mob guy but he was not connected to a crew and he was stupid. Dad would never have trusted him with anything at all. After a while, he drifted away and became the loser he was destined to be. The other guys were too scared to get too close to Dad and me. They thought if they sneezed the wrong way we'd kill them. I couldn't deal with them although one of them had a real nice Corvette that he used to let me drive. I guess he figured he could use it as leverage in case we decided to whack him. But we would never have bothered him. He was a gentleman. He just wasn't the one for my sister. Sally Boy fit right in with us. Sally Boy and I became instant friends and over the years we became as close as brothers. Both Dad and I have a deep love and respect for Sally Boy. Eventually, Dad made Sally Boy the business manager of the entire operation. It was a big job and Sally Boy was the best at it. He made a fortune for us, and all legitimately. This was an odd occurrence in our line of work.

Of course, my mom was beyond untouchable. People were afraid to look at her. Dad was having our house renovated in the 70s and every time Mom walked into a room, the workers would stop and tip their hats. My mom is not demanding, but these guys would fall over themselves trying to please her. They would have done anything for her because they knew she was *The Don's* wife. That made her a queen. She was treated like royalty everywhere she went. *No one wanted any trouble.*

Of the three women I have mentioned in this chapter, only my wife, Patty, a peace-loving soul who will rip your head from your shoulders if you piss her off, had to deal with a bit of fuckery. Those who knew that she was connected left her alone. They did not want a visit from Ice Pick Sammy or Jackie The Ripper, although she could have taken care of business herself. The hit men loved Patty because she was as fearless as them. But Patty did not work for the "family" business, at least for a time. She worked for a friend of my dad's, a doctor. She would take care of all the insurance business that doctors need to handle. That was her thing. For the most part, people were cool with her and when they were not, she could cool them out quickly. She had a way of chilling people out, even those who did not know that her father-in-law was *The Don* of a murderous crew of screwballs. One day, though, a bitch got on my wife's nerves.

The bitch was named Lexie and she was a pompous, self-righteous asshole. She wasn't a big shit corporate executive. She was just an administrative assistant. But Lexie gave Patty a hard time each time the two would speak. In the course of their jobs, they spoke often. Patty would be so upset she couldn't sleep at night. Lexie wasn't threatening Patty in any way. She was just being difficult and snotty. Now, my wife *never* asked my dad to kill anyone. She would have done it herself. It bothered me, though, to see Patty so troubled night after night. I don't know the details. All I know is that Patty would go on and on each night, almost to the point of tears. *That* was very unusual. I had never even met Lexie. In fact, I don't think Patty had ever met Lexie except on the phone. In any event, I decided to pay a visit to Lexie. I made an appointment to see the doctor for whom Lexie worked. I made up some bullshit story and the doctor saw me. Well, Lexie truly was a bitch. She was as rude and condescending to me as she had been to Patty. She wasn't unattractive but with an attitude like that I made up my mind that the world would be a better place without her.

I brought this business to Dad, who discussed it with Patsy. It was extremely unorthodox in the highly structured underworld but ultimately it was decided that it fell outside the realm of ordinary business. It was personal. This woman, Lexie, had insulted one of our own. Patsy adored my wife so he agreed with Dad. They put a contract out on Lexie. Her days were numbered.

The person who Patsy chose to do the hit was a heartless son of a bitch named Popcorn. Popcorn's specialty was psychological torture. The target was of no concern to him. The week before the hit, he planted a plastic explosive under Lexie's husband's car. It was wireless and could be detonated at any time as long as Popcorn was in close enough. He had done his homework and discovered that the husband picked up the kids from school every day at 3PM. He and Lexie had two girls, ages 7 and 10. Popcorn waited across the street from the school and at 3PM as scheduled, Lexie's husband rolled down the block. The kids bounced out of school and into the car and off they sped. I thought, *mission aborted: there are kids in the car.* I thought Popcorn was going to blast the car *before* the kids got in it. The car, kids and all, was halfway down the block and Popcorn pushed the button. The car went *BOOM.* I watched Popcorn's eyes. They were dead, unblinking eyes. He was absolutely emotionless as he did the deed. That fucking car became a flaming torpedo. It actually left the ground and surged forward, propelled by God only knows how much explosive power. Then it burst into flames. That was that. I think he took out some of the other kids and teachers and parents. I'm not sure. There were bodies everywhere. I don't know if they were alive or dead. I said to myself, *This motherfucker's nuts!*

Lexie was dumbfounded when she was told soon after. We all went to the funerals and consoled her. That's where Lexie finally met Patty. Lexie acted like an old friend and seemed grateful for Patty's words of condolence. But Popcorn just wanted to fuck with her before he killed her. She would be next. After the funeral, he gave her a few days to get settled, as if that were ever going to be possible. She was a broken woman and I began to feel allowing her to live would be more brutal than killing her. But she had to die. The contract was issued. These guys did not allow *anyone* to step on *any* of us, like you'd step on a doormat. When you put bad karma into the cosmos, you can *count* on it coming back to haunt you.

Lexie sat on the couch in her living room several weeks later. Things had calmed down. She was, perhaps, beginning to find some small measure of peace in her life. She was planning on moving out of the country and leaving all this horrible shit behind. It was late and she was watching *Late Night With David Letterman*, her favorite. She was relaxed for the first time in a long time. She didn't see Popcorn's rifle in the bushes outside her window, aimed just above the TV set. Popcorn had a high-powered scope on that fucking rifle. He took slow, deliberate aim. Letterman told a joke and before she could laugh, before she could even *blink,* there were six 22-caliber slugs in her head. Her eyes were taken out with sickening precision. The back of her skull was splashed against the wall behind her. It looked like a modern art painting. She slumped over onto her right side, still sitting in the same spot on the couch. What was left of her head came to rest on the throw pillow she fluffed a moment earlier. Letterman introduced his next guest.

Etymology

The etymology of the word Mafia is an interesting one. Loosely translated the word means "swagger." I often wondered why the mob guys walked as they did, with a bop in their step. They didn't walk all tight-assed, like the hen-pecked fools who ride the railroad to their stockbroker jobs everyday, the guys who follow the rules, pay their taxes, take shit from their bosses. Fuck them. The guys in the mob followed only one unwritten rule:

Sta Vitto! (Shut Up!)

Most monstrous of these guys, *The Dons*, the guys who order the murders, never come across as being tough guys. They certainly don't come across as stockbrokers, but they don't walk with the exaggerated swagger of the up-and-coming young hit men. Some of these older, grandfatherly *Dons* are the *most* ruthless, bloodthirsty, heartless killers. I have to laugh at the media in the USA today. Kids are taught that unless you are young, hip and beautiful (and stupid), you will be an unpopular wallflower who will never be happy and successful. I would *love* to find one of these "trendsetters". My 60 years on earth have afforded me the opportunity to learn countless ways to kill people and I would take great pleasure in dispatching one of these sack-less pieces of shit.

There was a young guy in the neighborhood back in the day. He thought he was King Shit. But he was just shit. His name was Monte. He had money and a straight job as some kind of corporate executive. His wife could have been a model. She was that beautiful. Her name was Monique. She probably could have been one if not for her and Monte's three little brats. They were obnoxious pains-in-the-ass. Whenever we were sitting in our lounge chairs in front of *The Little Shop of Insanity* and she would walk past, all eyes were on her. She had a fine ass. We all wanted to fuck her. But she wouldn't give us the time of day. To her, we seemed like *Bestia Feroce (Wild Animals).* That was too bad. Monte was a dick of the highest order. But we never bothered him. We would always mind our own business. He'd walk past the club and look at us with contempt.

One day one of the guys said to him, "Move to the suburbs."

Monte said, "Are you talking to me?"

We just laughed. We could have shot him 100 times before he hit the ground and not one person on the street would ever say he saw anything. We just ignored him. It drove us crazy thinking that Monte, the dick-less bastard, was tapping that most beautiful wife of his. Now that pissed us off more than anything. We were actually a peaceful lot as long as you did not fuck with us. When I say "us" I really mean "them". I was 17 years old. I wasn't a full-fledged member of the crew. I was a *Mobster-In-Training*. All I did was what the other guys told me to do, including threatening people's lives, roughing people up, dumping bodies, stealing, burning down buildings (for a number of reasons) and going to get the Chinese food.

Somehow, and I don't know where or when, Monte crossed the line. The guys weren't so forgiving anymore. If Monte would make a sound of disapproval as he walked by, which we always ignored in the past, the guys would erupt.

They'd jump out of their chairs and say, *"Vaffancuolo" (Go fuck yourself).*

I had heard rumors that Monte was borrowing money from the loan sharks in one of the other crews. Monte would look down at us because we were, in his opinion, mob scum, when all the while he was borrowing money from the mobsters in other crews. I guess his corporate job didn't cover the bills he had to pay in order to keep that fine wife of his happy. Apparently, he was very much in arrears and *The Big Dons* were tired of fucking around. A capo had sent a few guys to remind Monte that he owed them money. It was the usual stuff.

They'd say, *"Monte, you're a respectable guy. Pay us and we'll go away. No trouble."*

Why they didn't smack him around a little I'll never know. Monte would assure them that he would have the cash but he always missed his payments. These were serious guys he was fucking with. I guess he had more sack than I gave him credit for. He couldn't be that clueless as to think they would eventually go away. That was not going to happen. Since Monte lived by us, the other crews asked us to send him a serious message. The job fell to me.

My dad said to me, *"Don't hurt him, just blow something up."*

"OK, Pop," I said, always the dutiful, if a bit over-zealous son.

Hmmm. Let me give this some thought.

So I took a stick of dynamite and late one evening, when the neighborhood was quiet, I blew up his car. I had no idea that dynamite was so powerful. The blast obliterated the car, and blew a hole in the street. Plus, the flames shot in all directions and blew up two other cars. Pop said to blow something up! So I did. It must have done the trick, however. *The Big Dons* said that Monte made his next payment. But soon the payments stopped once again. The capo had run out of patience. He had some bone-breakers visit Monte and they put him in the hospital. The implement of destruction was a baseball bat. Monte's ribs were broken with a single, devastating blow. To the surprise of all the mob guys, Monte said he was going to bring a lawsuit against the entire lot of them. He was going to the D.A. When I heard this I said to myself, *"Arrivederci, Monte."*

This job was so big that all the crews joined forces. I got to watch but I really wanted to get in on the action. I hated that stupid prick. *The Big Dons* were so upset and fearful that this lawsuit would bring unwanted snooping by the authorities that they ordered a hit on Monte's entire family! Shit… I hated Monte's kids. They were creepy little bastards. But they were just little kids. I had no problem participating in the slaughter of guys, especially dumb fucks like Monte, but I didn't see the need to bring his family into the issue. However, *The Big Dons* gave the order: Monte and his family must die. *The Big Dons* were all close to 80 years of age. They looked like nice, gentle grandfathers but they pushed the button on the lives of children without batting an eye:

"Fuck them. Kill them all."

I see these young, make-believe tough guys in the media promoting their *"Young, Beautiful, Sexy, Bad Ass, ME"* images. It makes me sick. These 80-year old guys could roast those losers over an open spit, sprinkle some Bar-B-Q sauce on them and eat them. These were truly frightening guys. They might have looked like your Grandpa but they were evil motherfuckers. Let me tell you something, you stupid fuck: age does not matter. All that matters is balls. These 80-year-old guys had bigger balls than anyone.

My dad and Fat Patsy didn't care at all. These guys, *Il Capi Di Tutti Capi,* were among the most cold-hearted, brutal killers I had ever had the pleasure to know. I learned a lot during that meeting. As Fat Patsy would say:

"You gotta do what you gotta do. What could you do?"

I could feel the bloodlust growing within me. I was becoming a man. I had come to terms with murdering anybody who posed a threat to our way of life. The two crews made plans quickly. That very afternoon, when the family was out, they wired Monte's house with explosives. My dynamite slipup inspired them to put a charge big enough to flatten half the neighborhood. The family came home later that evening. The button man made sure that everyone was inside the house, and waited for everyone to go to sleep. It was 3AM when the charge was lit. The neighborhood was absolutely silent. Everyone was asleep, except us. It was as if an atomic blast was ignited. In an instant, Monte's house exploded up, sideways and down. The blast was so great it blew up the neighboring houses too. Three families died. The crews didn't care. The mission was accomplished.

The Big Dons were shaking our hands and saying:

Complimenti! (Congratulations!)

Ben Fatto! (Well Done!)

They were beaming.

Monte, his wife and his kids were reduced to ashes in a heartbeat. All that was left were some teeth and bones. The entire end of the block was in shambles. It was a crazy scene, very exciting. Fire engines raced up and down the block. Ambulances and police cars went screaming by. Everyone was awake and running around like lunatics.

But our job was done. It was time for us to go to sleep. It was late. We went home and settled into our beds. We didn't give it another thought.

The next day, I tried to walk past the blast site. It was roped off. But I could see from the corner that Monte's house, and the houses on either side of his, were gone. There were three giant craters were three houses stood. A total of 13 people died because Monte was a jerk. If he'd paid his debt none of this would have happened.

As my dad said, *"It's his own fault."*

Forgiveness

Forgiveness is overrated. When somebody pisses me off, which happens everyday, my immediate instinct is to turn the other cheek. I'll be the bigger man. Forgive and forget. I adopted this philosophy some years back, when I changed careers from mobster to musician. I am able to see the rage within artists who have this same philosophy. On the outside, they say, "It's cool, man." But a tempest rages within. I could never understand paintings that looked to me, at first glance, as if someone emptied the contents of paint cans all haphazardly on a canvas. For years, this art form made no sense to me. When I was running with Dad and his crew, if somebody pissed us off we killed him. It was clean, simple and easy: *Fuck me? FUCK YOU!*

Since I've become an artiste of sorts I try very hard to live a Godly life. I pray, I read the Scriptures and I try to be a blessing unto this earth every day. Oddly enough, now I see the angst in these modern, crazy paintings. They no longer look thrown together. To the contrary, they represent the inner turmoil that the artist is experiencing. I can see a deliberate hand at work. It's all because they turned the other cheek when someone stole their seat on the subway, or bumped into them without saying excuse me, or answered a simple question rudely. I'm not talking about serious crimes. I'm talking about the zillion moments each day when people have the option to be nice and they're scumbags instead.

I'm tired of turning the other cheek. I think that particular concept is way over-hyped. I really feel that it is much simpler to knock a guy's teeth down his throat than to say, "It's cool, man. I understand. You're having a bad day. It's no problem. You can be a rude prick to me. It's cool."

Forgiveness is bullshit.

People are generally pussies. You can fuck with them at will and they rarely say a word. I empower them to be rude to me by not kicking the shit out of them when they do so. I empower them to be inconsiderate when I do not unleash the wrath of hell upon them for their misdemeanors. Dad was right:

If you allow people to do it, they'll shit all over you.

I remember once back in the early 1960s, my dad and I went into a bar somewhere out on Long Island. He drank his usual rum & Coke and I drank my usual Coca-Cola. We decided to shoot some pool. I was 12 years old. There were two guys at the pool table and they had been there for over an hour. My father was pretty fucked up and my head was spinning from all the sugar in the five large Cokes I had downed. Dad walked over to the guys and said:

"Hey guys, would it be OK if my son and I used the table for a little while? You've had it for over an hour. We'd appreciate it."

I was surprised by my father's mild way on this evening.

One of the guys looks at my dad and says:

"You can have the table when we're finished."

To this, my dad replied as he chose a pool cue from the rack, his back to the wise guy:

"How about if I bash your skull in?"

My father cracked the pool cue in half over the wise guy's head. His head opened like a fucking cantaloupe and he collapsed on the table. Dad held the other half of the pool cue in his hand, like a dagger. He looked at the other guy and asked:

"Wanna play?"

"No, thanks," responded the freaked out character, and ran out the door.

The wise guy with the cracked cranium mumbled:

"Call an ambulance."

Dad spat on him and said:

"Call one yourself."

He pushed the motherfucker off the table and onto the floor. The guy actually dragged his ass to his car, blood gushing from an open gash on his head, and drove himself to the hospital. No one in the bar - it was almost empty anyway - even batted an eye.

I said, *"Dad, aren't you afraid he'll call the cops?"*

Dad said, *"No. He knows he's a dead man if he opens his mouth. Besides, ten to one he doesn't need some cop snooping into his business, just like this dump doesn't need the cops snooping around."*

Dad was my hero. Dad planted a seed at that moment that sprouted and still flourishes in me. Deep down, I fucking hate people. From that moment right up to this moment, there is that demon just beneath my civilized, calm exterior. The medication keeps the demon at bay, but there are times that even medication doesn't help. I hate people. I have no remorse for the guys I've beaten up. My only regret is that I didn't kill them.

I'm not sure exactly who wrote and edited *the Bible*. But I know it wasn't Jesus. I haven't read *The Cambridge History of the Bible* but I will. I do know that people had serious tempers 2000 years ago, just as today. Whether you believe that the Romans in conjunction with the Sanhedrin crucified Jesus or not, somebody crucified Him. I believe that The Lord is within each of us, somewhere deep inside. Therefore, I believe that The Lord is very much alive today. But if The Lord was a physical man again today, I wonder how He would react if someone spit in His eye? Would he say: "Spit in the other eye, My son?" Would He kick the guy in the nuts? Did Jesus get tired of forgiving people? He got pretty bugged when the moneychangers set up shop in the Temple. Who's to say what He would do now if some dickhead really got on His nerves? No, I cannot follow this Forgiveness vibe anymore. My patience has run out. My inner demon is knock-knock-knocking on Heaven's door.

If You Fell Into An Ocean Of Tits

My cousin, Angelo Ventura, is a muscle-bound, longhaired, black-belted career heavy metal musician who has spent the past 30 years touring the world with a variety of cult-favorite underground over-the-top super earsplitting rock bands. His body is covered with tattoos designed and inked by the legendary artist, Cuda Vendetta. He is also one of the funniest motherfuckers I have ever known and, thankfully, one of the most even-tempered. He is the brother I never had. We've been thick as thieves for our entire lives. He has a droll comment for just about every event in your life. For instance, for those who suffer from chronic bad luck, chronic stupidity or both, his pet saying is:

"If you fell into an ocean of tits, you'd come up sucking your thumb."

You have to love this guy. He is always laughing, always willing to lend you a hand and rarely in a bad mood, unless of course you abuse animals. Then he will turn his wrath on you. He and I were walking down a city street one day when we heard a dog yelping. Angelo ran over to a fence that shielded a vacant lot. He peered over the shaky wooden structure to see some loser beating his dog with a shovel. Angelo knocked the fence down with a single kick and before the shithead even knew what was happening, he planted his size 10 motorcycle-booted foot in the guy's face. The dog beater's nose and jaw shattered at once and he fell to the ground. Angelo checked on the pooch. Apart from a couple of bruises, the doggie was fine. Angelo adopted him then and there, naming him, aptly, *Pooch.* Then he walked back to finish the guy who was writhing in pain on the ground. I guess I could have saved the dog-beater's life the way Angelo saved Pooch's but I was enjoying the show. Angelo picked the guy off the ground and I held him up. He did a flying drop kick that sent the both of us hurtling back about five feet. I got up but the tough guy did not. Angelo had caved in his rib cage and stopped his heart with one devastating blow. We gave him a proper burial: we pissed on him. Angelo eschewed the mob life for touring in a metal band, but he would have made a hell of a hit man. Anyway, he picked up Pooch and put him in the car. We left the curled up, piss-covered piece of shit in the lot. I enjoyed watching Angelo kill that guy.

Another of Angelo's comic remarks involves young studs that think they are God's gift to women. My cousin has the rare distinction of having fucked women in every state of the USA, across Canada, South America and most of the free world. Conservative estimates hold that he has fathered 73 children but it's difficult to say. He keeps a low profile and it is very tough to bullshit him. One of the younger guys in his circle of friends is a sex addict and this annoys Angelo. It's like trying to brag about your slugging prowess to Mickey Mantle. Save your breath. Angelo had me rolling on the floor one night at a club when his I-Want-To-Fuck-Every-Woman-In-The-World buddy got on his nerves:

"You have pussy on your mind so much, your nose bleeds every 28 days. Give it a fucking rest, Don Juan."

That pretty much shut down Don Juan.

Angelo drove a muscle car. It was a 1970 Barracuda and was fast as the wind. I went for many a ride with him in that hotrod. Riding with Angelo took a strong stomach. He did 150 miles an hour on the open road. We'd cruise like that for the longest time. The police couldn't catch us, much as they tried. There was no other car that could keep pace with that Barracuda. Driving fast and playing bass are Angelo's two favorite things to do, although I prefer watching him kill people and then piss on them.

Recently, Angelo and I had lunch with my pal, Alphonse "Al Vegas" Moretti. He's another piece of work. There is a wonderful little Asian restaurant in town. "Vegas" loves it. We had a chill time talking about the old days. Like Angelo, Al Vegas is like a brother to me. He lives for his nightclubs. He is a tireless workaholic who puts in way too many hours. The good thing is that he owns a line of strip clubs across the country and especially in Las Vegas. From time to time the customers can get a bit out of hand, hassling the girls who work in the clubs. My dad is still connected, even now as he struggles with Alzheimer's in a nursing home. Al calls a phone number if the situation is too much for his bouncers. When he calls that number, the bad-boy customers are soon confronted with *real* bad boys. It only takes a couple of days for the bodies of the stupid bastards to be picked clean by the buzzards in the desert. Al Vegas doesn't fuck around.

Al Vegas and Angelo are not known as violent guys. They enjoy peace. They like to laugh and they are always willing to lend a helping hand to those in need. But if you push them, it will, most likely, be the last thing you do.

Mob Metaphysics

We all belong to a mob of some sort. We live in the real world. We exist. Even the members of the unbelievable, unrealistic world of professional sports or professional entertainment, where people "earn" in a day what for most folks is a year's salary, still breathe air, carry out the same bodily functions, experience somewhat the same level of emotion and arrange our lives in more or less the same manner as one another. Just as Aristotle wrestled with the notions of philosophy, wisdom and theology, we wrestle with the stress of day-to-day life: reason, logic and existence. We all do, we just do so in different ways. Some people write pop songs about absurdly simplistic concepts as love lost, love found and love making. While the term "pop" has its roots in the 1920s, first coined as "having popular appeal", it nonetheless means one thing: *dumb it down.* To reach masses, one must keep it simple. It is interesting to note that we all deal with far more complex issues every day of our lives: loyalty, courage, sacrifice, support, religion, and health to name but a few. However, our minds cannot easily and consciously grapple with these ideas. So we *dumb it down* as much as possible. This therefore makes such occupations as professional athletics and pop entertainers highly lucrative. I see the professional athletes and professional pop entertainers as greedy whores. The real thinkers, the owners of the teams, the owners of the global conglomerate entertainment companies and the like, are basically living in a multi-verse: they breathe the same air as us but that is about all they have in common with us. These folks are true mobsters, but they are seen as saviors, trendsetters, go-getters, doers, movers and shakers, and geniuses on a level of excellence that mere mortals can hardly dream of reaching. I see them as pimps.

What sets apart good earners from pimps and whores is the basic premise of humanity: share your blessings. Do you really think you're special because you can hit a baseball or play a guitar riff or sing a dumb ass pop song about your lack of civility, decency, depth or morals? *Fuck you.* What would make you special would be the humanity, kindness and caring that you could bring to people in need. Your money would go a long way in helping make a lot of souls happier and healthier. Once you've put out in that way, I really don't give a fuck if you buy a 6000-room mansion with 100 swimming pools. Once you have shared your blessings with your less fortunate brothers and sisters, with animals and with the Earth, then you have earned your wealth. Then you can be proud of yourself. Then you can expect continued blessings. It's all a matter of metaphysics.

It's simple: wrestle with it for a while and it will come to you.

This was never an issue with Fat Patsy, my dad and the crews all over the country. They took care of people. They gave away money, they spread joy and happiness. They fed people. They clothed people. They housed people. Even in the extreme, when a guy had to be whacked, they made sure that his wife and kids were financially secure for the rest of their lives. I see the above-mentioned entertainers and athletes in the same light that I see the mobsters: they are all in dirty businesses. But the mob guys make up for it, at least in some small measure, on a metaphysical level. They take care of the basics. They see to it that as many people as possible benefit from their "careers".

Logic is malleable in my opinion. What seems logical to you will probably seem impossibly illogical to me. I really find most people to be idiots. I suppose that is *my* problem. However, logic taken to extremes can truly convince the whore and the pimp that they are different from the mobster because what they do for a living is legal. *Bullshit*. I won't go into the extensiveness and pervasiveness of cheating and other illegal activities that take place in every facet of professional life, business life, political life, etc. *Please*. I see no difference between a pharmaceutical conglomerate holding back vital information on a drug that is supposed to cure people but instead kills people and a hit man who kills people for a living and makes no pretense to the contrary (such as the pharmaceutical conglomerates do).

It's simple logic: what is reasonable to you is unreasonable to me.

I offer no advice to the fuck-brains that skin people alive on a metaphysical stratum. *You'll get yours*. You are creatures of "now". Your just deserts will come later. You will swing from a velvet rope. You will dance with the devil forever and ever: *All'inferno (In hell).*

The Company Men

Some of the guys who worked for the record companies, "The Company Men", were the scum of the earth. They were snakes. They were far worse than mob guys. They were phonies. They were all thieves, they all cheated and they all lied. They dressed sharp, very expensively, but they were bums, lowlifes. The company men tried to make you believe they were not. They had secretaries and college educations and apartments in the high rent districts of Manhattan. They smiled and could be charming. But you could not trust them. You see, when a mobster points his gun at your head, he knows that he is affecting you in a negative way. There is no pretense. When a record company guy lies to you, steals royalties from you and ultimately drops you from his label due to "subpar sales", the damage to you is as real as a bullet to the back of the head. He just doesn't realize how devastating an affect he is having on you. It doesn't enter his mind. He is a self-centered, egotistical fuck-head that deserves to have his nuts cut off and shoved down his throat. I have come to realize that no one ever tells you the whole truth. Most people tell you most of the truth, but some people never tell the truth.

They smile and shake your hand: *"Hello! How are you?"*

But they don't even wait for an answer.

You could reply: *"Well, I'm dying of cancer, I'm fucking your wife and I'm going to kill you in your sleep tonight."*

These clueless ass-brains would answer: *"Great! That's nice to hear. Keep up the good work! Call me, we'll do lunch!"*

I have my gripes with artists but in a sense I can see why they are as nuts as they are. It's because they have to deal with clueless ass-brains!

I've had record company guys, "Executive Producers", tell me to turn down the bass, turn up the cowbell, and add handclaps. I don't tell them how to run their companies, but they have the contractual right to stick their long noses in my productions. I remember working at a studio in Nashville once. I was producing a bluegrass artist and the record company guy was breaking my balls all day. I finally snapped. There was a Tiffany chandelier in the lobby of the studio. It hung over a table low enough that you could read by it. You could reach up and touch it. I was sitting at this table and the record company guy was haunting me.

"Why don't we add strings to the track? I think strings would really make the track jump," he harped.

I was reaching the end of my rope: *"We are not using strings. This is bluegrass. It is traditional music. The artist does not want strings. If we add strings they will sound stupid, the artist will be unhappy, you'll lose a fortune and I'll quit."*

But the record company guy continued to push for the strings. I reached up and grabbed the Tiffany chandelier. I pulled with all my might and it came crashing down from the ceiling. I picked it up and threw it against the wall.

"I've had enough of this. Now either fire me or get the fuck out of my studio," I yelled, completely frustrated.

The guy chilled right out and actually started cleaning up the shards of broken glass. As he was doing so, he was apologizing.

"T-Man, we love you. I had NO IDEA you felt this strongly about it. No worries. The strings are OUT," decided the shit-brain.

Of course, after the record came out, I got a bill in the mail for the damage.

Still, relationships being as important as they are, I ate a lot of shit from company men. I was a jerk. I was a loyal motherfucker. I worked for low wages and long hours. I put up with bullshit from psychos of every description. Even though I was making a lot of money for their companies, they were not happy. It was almost as though they weren't doing their jobs if they weren't causing trouble. These guys could find fault in anything you did. I made some very famous records but the company men still found fault somewhere. They had no idea as to what they were doing. They looked everywhere for a problem. They looked everywhere but in the mirror. That's where the problem was. I worked hard at networking so I had more work than I could do. I worked constantly. Most of my productions had taken their places in musical history. But I was getting tired of fucking around with these bastards.

During this period in my life, 1988 through 2006, I worked every day, no vacations, no days off with the exception of a daytrip here and there. My enthusiasm for producing records was waning with each passing year. In 1990, I began teaching college as an outlet for my frustration. It was rewarding at first. But that too began to lose its luster over the years. I had a friend of mine in the mob, a guy named Zorro in the 1970s, who said to me:

"Trouble, unless you're working with your own crew, you're going to get fucked."

He was right. The Company Men, whether in the music business or the education business, have taken advantage of the loyalty that was ingrained in me from my birth. Zorro was murdered in 1980. But I think of him all the time. I think of his words and how right he was. My wife, Patty, became seriously ill in 2007 and it took three years for her to fully recover.

During that time, I spent every day with her and basically took all that time off from producing, touring and teaching. I needed to be with her and I was there for her every day. As I said, I am loyal. I came back to school to find a disturbingly large population of students who see themselves as hipper-than-thou. There are still those students who are truly good and soulful people. I stick with them. They make teaching worthwhile. I avoid the others. Everything is digital now. Records don't exist. CDs don't even exist. It's all digitally formatted. That's fine. That's progress. The Company Men are no longer an annoyance to me because I don't work for record companies anymore. The only artists that I produce now are D.I.Y. (Do It Yourself) artists. It's a different, and as far as I am concerned, better way to make music. I stay with my good friends and colleagues, some incredibly brilliant, helpful and kind people, and I avoid the people who are more ruthless than Jesse James. At this stage, I have plenty of money to live comfortably for the rest of my life and I don't need a job. I will work until it's not fun anymore.

When a company man no longer has you under his thumb, you have stripped him of his power. Follow your heart's desire, even if it means a lifetime of suffering. At least you'll have your pride. I'm inspired by my cousin Angelo Ventura, who passed up opportunities to work in the corporate world and make big money in order to pursue his dream of playing in his metal band. He's spent his adult life on the road, some 30 years (he's 50 now) playing small clubs for small money. He has sacrificed everything for his dream. It's not important if he achieves success on a grand scale because he's already achieved it within his soul. He wears 30 years of hard living on his face like a tribal mask. He is a warrior. He is who I will become.

Fuck The Company Men.

A Life In The Day

I was sitting on a bench at Grand Central Station, waiting for the 12:30AM express back to Port Jervis. I had a 2-hour train ride ahead of me and I was looking forward to a nice, long nap. Since Port Jervis was the last stop on the line, the conductor would wake me up when we arrived. It was a weekly routine with me. I live out in the boonies, in Pennsylvania across the Delaware River from Port Jervis, and the reggae band in which I play bass rehearses in New York City, right in Times Square. The train pulled into the station and opened its doors. I got up from the bench, slung my bass over my shoulder and boarded the train. I had my pick of the seats at this late hour and slumped down into a big, soft corner one. I placed my bass next to me and curled up in the seat, ready for a trip to slumber land. I didn't even notice the slight, frail figure enter the car and sit across from me. She startled me when she spoke, as I was beginning to drift off.

"I'm 166 years old," she said to me.

I opened my eyes and gazed at this wisp of a woman, barely five feet tall, barely 90 pounds. She had deep wrinkles across her forehead and down her cheeks, her hands shook slightly and her pure white hair fell in thin, straight strands down to her shoulders.

She had the brightest blue eyes I had even seen: *Oh, great. She's probably going to chew my ear off all the way to Port Jervis. It's just my luck to catch a wacko,* I thought to myself.

She probably saw me roll my eyes because a sly smile crept across her thin lips.

"I can see you don't believe me, young man," she said.

No one had called me "young man" in 40 years so she had my attention, at least for the moment.

"Excuse me, Madam, but I do not believe that you are 166 years old.

Perhaps you're 90 years old. But no more."

She glanced at me with a tilt of her head, *"Well, Sir, I must say that I have not received such a fine compliment in many a year,"* she said, just the slightest bit of coyness in her voice. *"In my day, I had my pick of gentlemen callers."*

Holy crap. Am I flirting with a 90 year-old woman? I mean, I'm not a kid but I'm a few years away from 90! *"I'm sorry, Madam..."* I started. *"Call me Minnie, that's my name. Minnie Chestnut,"* she said. *Minnie The Nut*, I am thinking:

"Excuse me. Minnie. But you can understand my skepticism. People just don't live to 166. 100 years is rare and this is 2012." She reached across and touched my arm with a bony hand and said:

"Lord knows, I have had my bouts with illnesses and accidents through the years. I have outlived everyone I knew for the major part of my life and I have been alone now for a good many years." At this point, I could see that she wanted to talk, that she was probably loony and that I was not going to get any sleep on this trip.

"OK, Minnie, do you have any proof of your age?" I asked.

"Oh, dear, yes," she said and produced a faded, barely legible piece of paper dated March 15, 1845. It was the Certificate of Birth of one Minerva Chestnut of Port Jervis, NY. She also produced photos of herself that were clearly very old. Although the girl in the photo was only about 15 years old, it was clearly Minnie. Those sparkling blue eyes were a dead giveaway. One could see by the young girl's sly smile that she was mischievous and more than a handful for her parents, whoever they were. She showed me several more. I have made a bit of a study of historic and aged photos and documents as part of my doctoral work and these photos were real. There was no doubt about it. *"This picture is one of which I am particularly proud,"* she beamed. It was the same young girl, now about 20 years old, blue eyes brighter than ever. She was taller, she had grown and stood about 5' 7", which was big for that era. The gentleman considerably taller, perhaps 6' 6", stood next to her.

"Do you recognize the man with me?" she asked.

My God! *"Minnie, this is Abraham Lincoln,"* I said, aghast.

"Yes, it is," she said. *"Mr. Lincoln was in Port Jervis in 1865 to preside over the war memorial that was erected in the town square,"* she explained. *"He was a very kind man and generously consented to take a photo with me when I asked him."* I knew that Lincoln did not travel with much protection and was often seen walking the streets of Washington alone. It is a well-documented fact that people came right up to him to shake his hand. So the fact that this young lady, whoever she was, could get her photo taken with him was plausible. *"He was assassinated by Mr. Booth a few weeks later. I cried for days,"* she said. This is bizarre. I am sitting here hanging on her every word, looking at a photo that is probably stolen or forged, and she's probably just escaped from an insane asylum. Yet, she captivated me. What was worse, I was beginning to believe her.

"I've outlived four husbands," she blurted out of nowhere. *Only four? "I married young the first time. I was 17. My husband's name was Jake and he was killed in the Civil War in 1862."* She fumbled around in her leather bag, clearly aged at least 100 years, and pulled out a photo of the girl with the blue eyes and a dashing young Union Corporal. On the back was written in black ink, now faded but clear, Jake & Minnie – our wedding day, 1862. My mind was whirling. Whatever was going on, I was in another time and space at this point. *"Jake is buried right in Port Jervis, in the old town cemetery. Go, have a look when you have a mind to do so."* Minnie explained to me that, after Jake died, she married again rather quickly, out of impulse, to a man much older than her. He was an importer/exporter and was worth a fortune, even by 2011 standards. He died of a heart attack soon after their marriage. I wonder how that happened: *I bet he croaked with a smile on his face.* Minnie was left a very rich woman. At the tender age of 18 Minnie Chestnut had five million dollars in the bank and was set for life, even if it lasted for 166 years.

Over the years, Minnie explained that she invested wisely and grew her fortune even more. By the turn of the 20th century she was worth ten million dollars. That's $10 million in 1900 money! She told me that she heard Caruso sing at the Vienna Opera House and that she met Mark Twain. *"I was here in your day too,"* she said. She had gone to Grey Towers in Milford, PA, for its dedication, over which President John F. Kennedy presided. Sure enough, she showed me a group shot in which she stood a few feet from JFK. You could see the Secret Service guys everywhere, unlike the Lincoln photo that was just the two of them. But there they were, JFK & Minnie, and a cluster of others, champagne glasses held in a toast. *I know what this is… some acid I must have dropped 40 years ago is just now kicking in…*

I didn't know what to believe. Minnie said that the other two guys she married only made her richer. They were both successful businessmen who died of heart attacks shortly after marrying Minnie. She was now middle-aged but still a handful, apparently. I asked her if her doctors had any explanations as to her reaching such an incredible age. "I don't believe in doctors," she said. "I've been sicker than hell over the years but I've always avoided doctors." She went on to say that she had met doctors from time to time at parties and social functions. As doctors will, they offered her unsolicited advice. *"Seven doctors told me to quit smoking cigarettes or I'd die of lung cancer,"* she said, *"and they're all dead."*

I became completely enthralled by her stories. Minnie was especially friendly with Amelia Earhart, although she avoided being seen with the aviatrix very much. They did not go out in public but preferred to spend quiet evenings at Earhart's Rye, NY, mansion. Read into that what you will, but I saw a few photos of Minnie & Amelia sitting on the front porch of the Victorian house on Boston Post Road. Again the paper, the apparent age and the feel of the pictures seemed right to me. I asked Minnie if I might possibly have one to show to a photo expert friend of mine. Minnie said she hadn't ever parted with any of her pictures. Minnie said she had been a close friend of Charlie "Bird" Parker, the famous jazz alto saxophonist. She showed me a photo of her with the legendary musician sitting at a table at The Cotton Club. I could believe that she might have sat at a table with Bird but I could not believe that she was a friend of his. *"Oh, my,"* Minnie said as I stared awestruck at the picture, *"Bird was a darling. He even gave me this reed which he signed and if you flip the picture over you'll see it's autographed."*

Being a musician myself, and holding Charlie Parker in such high esteem as I do, it was just a bit too much for me to buy. She might have infiltrated the inner circles of President Kennedy and Amelia Earhart, and she might have even been granted a photo op with President Abraham Lincoln, but there was no way Minnie Chestnut could have been a confidant of the late genius Charlie Parker. Out of curiosity, I flipped the photo and sure enough it was signed, "To my dear friend Minnie, with love from Charlie Parker." She showed me the reed and there faded along the back of it was the identical "Charlie Parker" signature. This was more than I could bear so I asked if I could snap a picture of the picture with my cell phone camera. She obliged and I took photos of the front and back including the signature, as well as a photo of the reed. I happened to have a friend who worked at the Smithsonian and I texted the pictures to him. His specialty is identifying historic artifacts and he had the means with which to do it. His lab boasted the latest in such technology. I knew if he had a bit of downtime, he would help me with this mystery. My phone rang a mere 15 minutes after I sent the texts.

"Where did you get these pictures?" he asked.

"I snapped them with my cell phone, the originals are in a lady's bag. She's sitting across the aisle from me on the train," I said.

"Well, my friend, the Parker autographs are authentic," he announced, a touch of excitement in his voice. He went on to say that the reed had indeed once belonged to the Bird.

"How on earth can you tell that?" I asked, almost wanting him to have been mistaken.

"Bird used custom-made reeds, with special symbols on them," my friend at the Smithsonian said. *"The symbols are code for the date of manufacture and the artisan who made them. No one knew this, not even Bird. No one could possibly have copied this reed, it is the real thing,"* my friend said.

I decided to text him a picture of the JFK photo. Minnie was by now amused to see me jumping through hoops. Sure enough, that was JFK, and his signature was authentic. So I went for broke and texted the Lincoln photo. *No way this is real*. It's got to be a computer mock-up. When my phone rang I was a bit hesitant to answer. My friend barked at me in a snide voice, *"Are you kidding?"*

"What?" I asked.

"This is a famous photo. There are no unknown photos of Lincoln. People didn't walk around snapping pictures with cell phones back then. Lincoln took his personal photographer, Alexander Gardner, with him on road trips."

WHAT? It seems that copies of this particular photo of Minnie & President Lincoln are actually on display in a number of historic locations, including the Smithsonian. But the original has long since disappeared.

"Well, I found it," I said sarcastically.

Now it was my friend's turn. *"WHAT?"* Yes, I said to him, I had indeed found the original photo. *"Where is it?"* he asked anxiously. *"In Minnie's purse,"* I said. *"Minnie who?"* he asked. *"Minnie Chestnut,"* I said nonchalantly.

"Minnie Chestnut, the lady in the photo..." my Smithsonian friend said, with more than a bit of derision in his voice. *"Yep,"* I said as Minnie read the newspaper, paying no attention whatever to me.

"You realize, my delusional friend, that Minnie Chestnut would be, what, 166 years old now?" my increasingly cynical friend said. I reminded him that it was he who proved her age by authenticating the historic artifacts I texted to him. Perhaps he was not so much the "authority" as his diplomas and awards stated? Perhaps he was a bit overrated in his field? I thought he was going to blow his top. There was little doubt that Minnie was who she said she was. I stared out the window, my mind reeling but strangely settled.

As the train pulled into the Port Jervis station, the last stop on the line, I gave my arm to Minnie and she took it. I walked her out of the car and onto the platform. She kissed me on the cheek and said, *"Thank you."*

"It was my pleasure, Minnie Chestnut," I said, as she went her way and I went mine.

Misadventures In Teaching

Up until 1990, if anyone told me that I would someday be a college professor I would have said that he was crazy. Considering the way in which I started life, teaching anybody anything except how to steal, cheat and lie was not something of interest to me. I basically hated people. I don't really know how this teaching thing got into my head. I have a friend who is a college professor and I mentioned to him that maybe I'd like to teach. The thought materialized from thin air. He hooked me up. Next thing I knew, I was teaching music at a local college. It seems my experiences in the music business were of interest to students. For the longest time, years and years, it was cool. But as the computer age brought a whole new crop of know-it-all unhip hipsters to the school, my feelings of love, as with most other areas of my life, began to turn to disgust. Where students used to be extremely interested in the records that I produced - eclectic, grassroots, non-commercial albums by a variety of world-renowned artists - now all that matters to many students is what other clueless fuck-heads tell them is hip. Music, like everything else in the world, is quickly eddying down the toilet. While there are those students who truly understand what I am saying, that we create art for its own sake, that life is fragile and an ill-considered comment can ruin a life - many, I am sad to say, have no idea how to live and how to interact with others. In order to reach these people, I have to defer to their way of thought or at least try to understand it, treat them with courtesy and kindness and swallow my pride the way a *puttana* (whore) swallows a mouthful of cum.

A spoon-fed, whiter-than-white boy said to me recently, *"You are a dinosaur from the 60s. Nothing you have done in your career has the slightest relevance in my life."*

As I have done a hundred other times, I let it go. But my inner rage builds.

Sometimes my students were junkies. I hold no revulsion towards them. They can't help it. They're fucked up. When they lie to me, I expect it. I do my best to straighten them out. These guys are actually much more caring than the spoiled babies who are clean, straight and defective. They walk around with their noses glued to iPods and other such mind-numbing devices. They talk incessantly on their cell phones. They *Twitter* and *Facebook* and whatever the hell else they consider hip but they have no social skills. They do not smile and I doubt they know how. They walk around with earplugs blaring this God-awful crap "music" into their wax-clogged ears. I fucking loathe these fools. Their parents are older versions of them. Inconsiderate, unaware, pampered pieces of human garbage. It is baffling to me that these stupid kids think they have gotten more experience at 20 years of age than I and my colleagues have gotten in 60 years. They have no track records at all. They have done nothing except jerk off to internet porn. They are afraid of their own shadows. Because I have allowed myself to take their shit for so many years, I hate myself as much as I hate them. By age 20, I had been involved in every kind of illegal activity from robbery to attempted murder. My friends were the scariest motherfuckers on earth. I have seen people slaughtered right before my eyes and I have not flinched. I enjoyed watching their agony. I enjoyed inflicting pain. I was surrounded by brutality. I learned to fear no one. I learned to respect no one except for the people in my crew. My Godfather is a *Don*. My father is a *Don*. I will no longer allow these fuck-brains to test me. I will open the gates of hell. I will ride a Pale Horse of my own. My fury will chase them down.

The Port Jervis Professor

Recently, my wife and I moved to Pennsylvania. The pace of life is slower there. We like it a lot better than in Westchester County, NY, the "Me First" capital of the world. Still, I maintain a busy performing and teaching schedule and I spend many hours each week driving and riding the railroad. I thought it might be easier to catch the train in Port Jervis, NY, just across the Delaware River from PA, than to drive to Westchester to catch the Metro North to Grand Central Station. So one Sunday afternoon my wife and I drove over to Port Jervis to look for the station. We soon found what looked like an abandoned depot. There were empty, old wooden structures, railroad cars that, by the look of them, had been retired in the 1950s, rusted tracks that led to dead ends and not a soul around… except for one man, a portly, bearded, balding gent who looked to be in his sixties. He had a camera and was shooting photos of the classic railroad cars that sat, unattached and unused, everywhere. "Excuse me, Sir," I called. He turned, smiled and walked over to my car. "I was wondering if you might know where the Port Jervis station is. By the look of this place, this can't be it," I said. "Well, this was the Port Jervis station for almost 100 years, from just after the turn of the 20th century until 1993," the man said. "As a matter of fact, two presidents, FDR and JFK, stopped at the Port Jervis station on their ways to Milford, just across the bridge." "Interesting…" I said but before I could say another word the man continued. "You know, there are other Port Jervis stations in the USA, one is in the Appalachian Mountains!" "I didn't know that," I said, still trying to have my original question answered. "Oh, yes, to be sure," the man said. "In fact, there was a Port Jervis Railroad Line that ran from Tuscon to San Francisco but of course came nowhere near Port Jervis, NY," he said. "That old car right there," he turned and pointed to one of the classic beauties rusting away in what was once a busy train yard, "ran on that line." I looked and sure enough there it was printed across the side, Port Jervis Railroad Line, Tuscon, Arizona. It seems that I had happened upon an historian, a fount of knowledge regarding railroads in the United States. Judging by the dissertation I was hearing, I had the feeling that I could make an educated guess as to this gent's occupation.

"You wouldn't by chance be a college professor, would you?" I asked.

"Why yes!" he said, "How on earth did you know?"

"Oh, just a lucky guess," I said.

The Professor did not miss a beat as he continued his dissertation. He named the various stops on the Port Jervis, NY, line, and just about every other U.S. line that had a Port Jervis station. He orated on the origin of the name Port Jervis in New York and even knew the names of a few of the conductors and engineers going back to the turn of the 20th century. By this point, I was beginning to feel that it was about time for class to be dismissed. "Professor," I said, "your monologue on the history of the Port Jervis railroad lines in the U.S. is truly fascinating but I was wondering if you would tell where the current Port Jervis, NY, station is located." The Professor stroked his beard and gazed off in the distance, as if pondering the question. I stared at him expectantly. Finally, with a somewhat puzzled look on his face he said, "I haven't a clue." I was surprised by his candor.

College professors can be Know-It-Alls. It's rare to hear one say that they do not know something. However, before I could savor the moment, The Professor was back in the game. He began to tell me the most ridiculously outrageous tales, ones that simply could not be true. For instance, The Professor began rattling off a number of famous people who were, according to him, his former students. Presidents, CEOs, artists and more had all apparently studied with him, meaning that he would have had to teach in some 50 colleges worldwide. This was a bit of a stretch and I was beginning to tire of his overt fabrications. Then he said his great, great, great, great Grandfather was a Mayan chieftain and that royal blood flowed in his veins. "Oh man let me out of here," I thought to myself. But then he uttered something that really got my attention. He said to me, "You know, I recently bought an old house here in Port Jervis and I found the oddest thing in the attic." I was about to say that my wife and I had to get going, but something he said caught my ear.

"I believe that I have a recording embedded in the decorative grooves of a very old clay pot." He went on to say that he believed within the grooves of that clay pot was embedded the voice of Mozart.

WOLFGANG AMADEUS MOZART?

The Professor said that he had a friend who was a bit of an inventor. This gentleman had built a machine especially to play the clay pot. "It was more of a lark than anything else," he said.

However, when the two eccentrics tried out the new invention, they were sure that they heard a voice say the name Mozart.

I explained to the Professor that was in my area of academia now. I've been producing records for 30 years and teaching music for 20. I told him so. But strangely enough I had heard of such things. I had not seen or heard them myself. Still it was a hot topic. The Professor offered to show me the clay jug and I decided to take him up on it. He did not live far from where we stood so we walked the few blocks to his house.

The house was a rambling, crumbling, lopsided, once-beautiful-but-now-unsightly pile of lumber more than a century old. He had made no attempt to renovate the place, the inside being as shabby as the outside. Still, it had a charm and my wife and I were comfortable there. We walked up the creaking stairs to the attic. There we found the clay pot. It was kept just as it had been found, in a wooden box clearly over 200 years old.

"Have you tried to listen to the pot more than that one time?" I asked. He said he had not.

I went for broke and asked him if I might borrow the urn for a few days. I confessed to him that I, too, was a college professor and that I had access to equipment on which we might be able to "play" the pot. I invited him to attend all meetings and sessions so that the pot would not leave his sight. He agreed immediately. I made an appointment with a friend and colleague of mine, Dr. Peter Barron. When the date rolled around, the three professors met and studied the clay pot. Professor Barron indicated that the pot could not be played in the traditional sense but that he had developed a computer program that would be able to extract information that could be read, ergo, "played". Professor Barron put the pot into a CAT scanner that he had modified for such purposes as reading unplayable, scratched and otherwise broken records. We watched in awe as the computer monitor in front of us actually spewed out data!

"Well," Dr. Barron said, "the grooves on this pot definitely contain data. I'm sure it was put there unintentionally. Nonetheless, it's there."

Professor Barron transferred the data to a recording application and within minutes we were listening to sounds that would forever change our lives.

"Mozart," we heard, *"ist das richtig?"*

WHAT?

"Nein," we heard.

Was this the voice of Mozart?

"Überschnell," the voice said.

Was Mozart telling someone that he was playing a piece too quickly? My God, what have we discovered?

"Scheißen," said another voice.

SHIT? How weird is that? We were listening to a recording of a guy who lived in the late 18th century saying *"Shit."*

We analyzed the entirety of the data. We could actually hear Mozart and company playing a piece of music. It went on for about 30 seconds.
I am not an expert on Mozart but I do know a good bit about the brilliant composer. I had studied his work in college. I was, however, unaware of the brief snatch of music that Dr. Barron had gleaned from the clay pot. I asked another colleague of mine, Dr. Brooke Bradford, to listen to our discovery. As he did so, Dr. Bradford paled, almost swooned and damn near fainted:

"Gentlemen," he said after regaining his composure, *"this is a section of Mozart's Lost Sonata."*

He continued that it was believed that Mozart had composed the piece but to date no music had ever been found. For over 100 years, classical musicians had been performing what they believed to be a Süssmayer variation of a Mozart theme that was, perhaps, akin to the "Lost Sonata".

"This is beyond belief, gentlemen," Dr. Bradford said.

Apparently this discovery proved that for 100 years, everyone has been performing the wrong composition. They were not performing the "Lost Sonata" at all. God knows what the hell they were performing. *WELL, WHAT DO WE DO NOW?* The four genii looked at one another for a long minute. There was only 30 seconds of music. No one would dare finish it. The classical press is brutal. It would be an insult to the memory and music of Mozart. At once, inspiration struck. The four educators looked at one another and knew that each was thinking the same as the next. Mozart would LOVE this. A little-known fact is that all four men, in chatting idly before the session began, discovered that they all loved Jamaican dancehall music. Mozart was a prankster. That is a known fact. What better way to utilize this precious find than to sample it and produce a hit record? So the four comedians contacted a famous music producer, Prince Phillip, and asked him to go to work on it. The Prince brought in equally famous reggae stars, Jay & The Dread Zones. Within weeks, the reggae dancehall track, *Me Fi Dem Wolf Gongs*, was number one on the reggae charts across the USA, the Caribbean and Europe, including Mozart's hometown of Salzburg. Mozart himself was the pianist on the record.

In the midst of it all, late at night, while his old town slept, the Port Jervis Professor tapped his foot to the big beat, his console stereo unit pumping the jam into the humid, still night air. This was undeniable: he was part of it. His heart was at peace for the first time since God knows when.

Ties

There are different kinds of ties. These include:

Neck Ties

Ties That Bind

Ties That Break

Sports Game Scores

Tie Receptors

Blood Ties

Musical Notation

Tie Connectors

Railroad Ties

The list goes on and on.

The kind of tie that I discuss here, however, is the Time Tie: the thing that is our common denominator. I refer to Death. It's the one thing that we all do, no exceptions. I realize that the younger one is, the more remote the idea of this particular common denominator seems. I know that, indeed, some younger people feel that they will never die. I'll take that bet. Son, you are a walking dead man. You might as well get used to the notion. I cannot understand why the youth walk around feeling depressed or invincible or too high or too low or medicated. The 70's must have produced a bunch of junkies or idiots or both because their children are fucked up. The idea is to "live now". Enjoy the gift of life that you have been given. Life should begin and end with a smile. It should be a wonderful addiction. Instead, it has been reduced to something that must be done. All I see as I walk the streets are distant, poker-faced, yellow-veined, heartless humanoids. Some of them are pretty to the eye but all of them are damaging to the soul. The idea of catching a warm breeze in the palm of one's hand is alien to these people. They are tied to nothingness. They are tied to less than nothing. They are homeless in their minds. They are soulless. There are no chemicals that can repair their broken spirits. They dwell in stolen cars lit by computer screens and cell phones. They shake like leaves on ancient skeleton trees. They exist in a strange place within. The cure is sure: the way to do is to be (Lao Tzu). These people are tied to nothing, to no one. They think they know but they don't know.

The mob guys with whom I spent my youth may have been a lot of things, including murderers, but they had ties. They taught me, oddly enough, to appreciate life, to be thankful for all that I have been given and they taught me to dream, even if no one else believes in you. There is something utterly magical about dreaming a dream that no one else but you can see. There is something wonderful about reaching for a goal that everyone else thinks is unreachable. I learned this from a bunch of ruthless killers, pimps, pushers and thieves. These guys had soul. If you belonged to their world, no matter the crew, you were tied to all of them. If you didn't belong to a crew, they left you alone at least, but were always willing to help you. They could stop your heart with a fierce look but they never looked anything but happy to see you. It was a rare occasion that they ever gave anyone that look. They threw parties far more than they killed people. They hugged everyone.

Today's youth link only to themselves. They stand within forests of skyscrapers but they realize nothing. They look but they do not see. With eyes wide open, they are blind. They hang limp, like puppets, from strings held by convention, the media and dick-head suits. They do not hug. They are not comfortable displaying any emotion except anger, when they can muster the courage to show even that. They thrust their fish hands out, but it's just a formality. They stare at me blankly. They are robots tuned to a nonexistent wavelength. They are clueless. They are wrecks. The forest floats as predators emerge. They are vulnerable. In the blink of an eye, they are gone. A vampire wind bites their necks. They are under its spell. They battle in their quiet places. They tell me to mind my own business but they are my business. So I tie myself to them, and I hope that someday they will grow a soul.

To quote my dad:

Chi mangia solo crepa solo. (He who eats alone dies alone.)

Bullshit

The *Little Shop of Insanity*, in addition to the parties, card games and murders that were held there, was the site of some of the most enormous piles of bullshit ever crapped out by the demented mind of humankind. A number of the guys who frequented the club could easily have been stand-up comics. They kept me laughing almost all the time. Some of them intentionally told very tall tales, knowing well that no one believed them. They were just spinning yarns for our entertainment, nothing more. There was a guy named *Regular Vinnie.* We called him that because we had three *Vinnies* in our crew: Big Vinnie, Little Vinnie and Regular Vinnie. The latter kept us raft as he told the most incredible stories, obviously fiction. Nonetheless, his delivery was such that one could never quite be sure. Regular Vinnie once said that his dog, Phoebe, was an alien from outer space. He said that a spacecraft landed in his expansive backyard in rural upstate New York and entrusted Phoebe to him. As payment for this great favor, Regular Vinnie would be the only human assured safety when the aliens invaded earth. Regular Vinnie said that the world was going to be under siege on April 1st. There would be squadrons of UFOs shooting laser death beams effectively flattening the earth and leaving it in ruin. All traces of life would be gone. However, since they were leaving Phoebe with him, (and by the way, Phoebe was the leader of the invading alien forces, a race of dogs) the destiny of the entire world depended on Regular Vinnie. If he could dissuade Phoebe, who was directing the operation from Regular Vinnie's house, then perhaps he could save the world. Regular Vinnie thought that maybe a *boy dog* would keep Phoebe busy and she wouldn't want to destroy the earth. So he went to the dog pound and brought home the most attractive male dog he could find. The dog was a mix, German Shepherd and Irish Setter. His name was Big Foot, but he was well endowed in other areas as well. Phoebe took one look at her new dreamboat doggie and called off the invasion. All she wanted to do was live in peace and start a family with Big Foot. Regular Vinnie and his quick thinking had thwarted certain destruction and preserved life on earth.

"What the hell are you talking about?" said one of the guys who had been listening in an almost trance-like state, *"April 1st passed months ago!"*

"See?" said Regular Vinnie, *"That proves I saved the world!"*

This would be met with rounds of *"Get the fuck outta here,"* and, *"You're a bat shit crazy motherfucker."* But everyone laughed and clapped. Once again, Regular Vinnie had spun the web and we all found ourselves ensnared.

My dad would always say such pearls of wisdom as:

"If you have money, tell people you're broke. If you're broke, tell them you have money." It's based on lies, but lies for the purpose of achieving an end. I never knew when my dad was telling me the truth or lying to me. But it wasn't to impress me with feats of greatness that he had not performed. It was to get something done, to reach a goal. It was business. That was fine with me. Dad gave me a skill that I use to this day.

Others were shameless liars. They were braggarts. They want to impress people with feats that they did not perform. The words they spoke were beyond bullshit. These guys were embarrassments to themselves and to us. There was a difference between bullshitting to get something done and bullshitting to boost your own ego, impress someone or take credit for something you did not do. The latter form of bullshit was one upon which the mobsters frowned. In extreme cases, it could get a guy killed. It meant that he had a big mouth and could not be trusted. Remember the rule: *Sta Zitto. Shut up.*

There was such a character, named Skutch, in the crew. He could not tell the truth. He knew Mickey Mantle. He knew Marilyn Monroe. He killed 52 guys (who all happened to live in other parts of the country and no one had ever heard of any of them). He was a jive motherfucker and it was tedious work to be around him. I am sure that this is where my impatience with bullshitters took root. Everyone avoided him. He really had no job or responsibilities. When he walked into the club, no matter what fun stuff was happening, it was time to sing "The Party's Over". Usually, such guys would be told to leave, in no uncertain terms. This was always the case with Skutch. But on one occasion Skutch dropped the mother lode of bullshit. In an effort to make himself seem important and to perhaps, believe it or not, threaten Fat Patsy, of all people, Skutch said:

"I am personal friends with the D.A. He's been asking questions but I told him you guys were OK. I said to the D.A. 'Patsy is a close friend and he's a straight-arrow guy.'"

Patsy didn't even reply. He just laughed and walked away. Skutch laughed too and flopped down onto an easy chair as if he didn't have a care in the world. But Skutch had finally taken his fantasies a bit too far. I saw Patsy's eyes as he turned his back on Skutch. They were almost glowing red. If he was ever angrier, I had not seen it. I knew that Skutch was going to die. I had a feeling that it would be soon. At the moment this incident took place, I was the only other one in the club. I saw Patsy go into the back room and make a phone call. Within a few minutes, five or six hit men entered *The Little Shop of Insanity.* There was no small talk, which usually preceded a hit. They pounced on Skutch who was in shock in an instant. They held him down as I watched Patsy walk slowly and calmly to Skutch. Skutch was screaming. Patsy beat the shit out of Skutch to cool him down, punching him in the face time and time again. There was blood everywhere. But Patsy had not delivered the final blow. Once Skutch was stunned into submission, Patsy brought out the biggest pair of gardening shears that I had ever seen. He snapped them in Skutch's face. Then one of the guys grabbed Skutch's tongue with a pair of pliers. Patsy, shears in hand, severed Skutch's tongue. Skutch howled and gurgled as the blood oozed down his chin and cascaded down his throat. The guys dragged Skutch, who was still very much alive, into the back room and placed him face down over the drain in the floor. The blood flowed directly into the drain and that meant less cleanup time for me. Skutch died a slow, painful, agonizing death. When the end finally came for Skutch, Patsy said, *"What's that sound? Oh wait, it's silence!"* We threw Skutch's body out back and covered it with a tarp. Then, late that night, I recruited a few of my friends to help me chuck the corpse into the Long Island Sound. We had a boat for just such chores that we drove to a pitch black, desolate spot off the shoals off Orchard Beach. We knocked the corpse's teeth out to eliminate dental records and we smashed his face into a pulp. We stripped it and took the ID. Then we weighted it down with bar bells and chains and dumped it over the side. It sank in an instant. That was the end of Skutch, master bullshitter.

I know people today, as I try to navigate my way through life, who bullshit even more than Skutch. These guys would not have lasted long back in the day. We should be happy with who The Lord made us to be, whatever the career path or vocation. We cannot be who we are not. We cannot live fiction. We cannot put fiction into the cosmos. It will come back to us in a bad way. Skutch did and look what happened to him.

Money

It is the root of all evil and the one thing that everyone wants, needs and never has enough of, even when one has more of it than anyone could ever spend in a lifetime. It's Money. People have died from lack of it and because of it. People steal it, hide it, hoard it and have it. People need it, fuck for it, get fucked for it, and get fucked because of it. Some people even kill for it.

There is nothing a mobster wants more than money, except power. The same holds true for politicians, Wall Street brokers, CEOs, entertainment business shitheads, entertainers with giant egos, and dickhead athletes who make zillions of dollars for playing games. But money and power usually go together so the point is rather moot. In a sense, I guess I have always been a hippie because I have never lusted for money. I've always worked hard to make enough money to pay my bills and maybe save a few bucks. But I've never screwed anyone over for money and I've never been a workaholic for the sake of money. However, I used to work for guys who would kill you if you screwed them over money. If a guy was stupid enough to try to get away with putting one over on Fat Patsy, then *fu ucciso (he was killed)*. It was only business as far as he was concerned. Watching these murders was big fun. It was like watching TV only this was real life. The guy would finally figure out, after a few minutes of small talk, that *stava per morire (he was about to die)*. He would beg for his life but his pleas fell on deaf ears. Then, if he was lucky, the hit man would pump one slug into the back of his head and it was over. If he really fucked up and Patsy was especially angry, it might take all day to kill him. I've seen guys taken apart, literally, piece by piece

As the Bicentennial approached in the USA and the disco era was in full swing, I was enjoying my new career as a professional, albeit poor, musician. I was a live-and-let-live kind of guy. I was trying to be one, at least. I would still work for my dad from time to time but more in a "bookkeeping" capacity. I would pick up gambling receipts from the various bookies that worked for Dad and Patsy and I would bring the money to *The*

Little Shop of Insanity. Sometimes I would have a quarter of a million dollars in an A&P shopping bag. God help the bookie whose figures didn't tally. I look back upon those days now with a sense of awe. I carried all that cash in a paper bag and no one dared to touch me. Everyone on the street knew that I had mega-bucks in my shopping sack and I was walking and alone to boot. If a *cugino (cousin, i.e. mob guy)* dared fuck with me, his life would be measured in minutes. The bookies ran their businesses out of the most bizarre locations: barber shops, delicatessens, pizzerias and even funeral parlors. I remember visiting a bookie at his funeral parlor to pick up the week's receipts. As we sat in his office and he compiled the tickets and filled my shopping bag with cash, he asked me if I heard that "Meatball" got whacked. He said Meatball was laid out in the "A" Suite if I wanted to see him before the family got there.

I said, "Sure. I knew Meatball."

What the bookie didn't know was that I was there when Meatball got sent to Heaven. I don't know why he was killed, but Patsy pushed the button on him. As I said, I just went along to watch. The dead mobster was a friend of Patsy's until he crossed him somewhere along the line. I stood at Meatball's coffin and looked down at him. He had taken it like a man and said to let Patsy know there were no hard feelings. He knew he fucked up. *Caspita! (Good God!)* Oh well, my shopping bag loaded, I strolled out the door onto the sun-drenched street.

I spent many a lonely hour in my tiny apartment when my first wife left me. I am a very picky person when it comes to women. Just as I prefer inner peace in lieu of a fat bank account, I prefer intelligence, charm and wit instead of beauty if I have to choose. I lucked out with my second wife Patty, to whom I remain married after 30 years. She has it all. So although I dated quite a bit, I could not bear the company of an idiot, even if she had giant boobs. After all, my dad bought a prostitute for my 16th birthday. I had gotten, as my good friend Jackie The Ripper would say, "Wild & Crazy" for a good number of years by this point. I really longed for the company of a sensitive, bright, witty down-home type girl. In cases such as this, money is not an important factor. A poor musician can offer only his love and perhaps a home cooked dinner courtesy of Chef Boy-R-Dee every now and again. Until I met Patty, such women did not exist as far as I could see. The women I dated, actresses, singers, and artists - women one would think would be my heart's desire - were into expensive dinners, expensive concerts, expensive Broadway shows, expensive gifts, expensive cars (not 1976 Honda Civics), expensive vacations and *money*.

Money is a unit of account.

Money is a store of value.

Money is a standard of deferred payment.

Money is a medium of exchange.

You have commodity money, representative money, fiat money, commercial bank money and currency. You have dirty money, clean money, cash, checks and IOUs. The love of this stuff boils down to one word: *Greed*. Scavengers, hoarders, pirates, devils, pigs and scumbags of every description condemn the eternal things for the temporal things. Fucking narcissists. Just as the boy in the Caravaggio painting got his for love of self (love of temporal things), so will every greedy motherfucker who cuts the line, snubs, looks down upon, condescends, flashes his material stuff and rejects the spiritual.

I give a lot of money away these days. I give a lot of my possessions away as well. I try not to become overly fond of material things. I don't collect anything. I think it is important to move, relocate, so as not to become too comfortable in this material world. I am searching for that peaceful place in my soul where I can live forever. I am sickened by what I see in the media. I am sickened by the bullshit that passes for importance in this media-driven, money-hungry global society. If you are slim, young, beautiful, self-absorbed, stupid, possess the correct cell phone and computer and, oh yes, possess lots of money, then you will be happy. What they are really saying is: if you choose to give up your freedom for wealth, power, beauty and eternal youth, then you will be happy.

Jesus said, "If you wish to be complete, go and sell your possessions and give to the poor, and you will have treasure in heaven; and come, follow Me." But when a young man heard this statement, he went away grieving, for he owned much property. And Jesus said to His disciples, "Truly I say to you, it is hard for a rich man to enter the kingdom of Heaven." ***(Matthew 19:21-26)***

The Dotted Line

I always saw myself an outlaw biker, living outside of society, living on the road, tied to no one, caring for no one. I saw myself striking fear into the hearts of all with whom I came in contact. I saw myself to be unmoved by life, an enigma on a Harley, a gangster, a bad guy. I saw myself as a guy who didn't give a damn about anything. Daddies lock up your daughters. I wanted to kill people, as the song goes, "…just to watch them die." I wanted to be feared.

I wanted the devil to worship me.

I wanted to hate people. I wanted to leave a bloody trail of death and destruction and chaos in my wake. I would turn my wrath and rage upon anyone who fucked with me. I would take advice from no one and I would seek advice from no one. I would be made of stone. I would tolerate no weak shit from anyone anywhere. My tattooed chest would read:

Fuck Everybody

But somewhere along the way, I signed on the dotted line.

I earned several scholastic degrees including a Ph.D. I find it impossible to hate people and very easy to love people. I cannot ride a motorcycle. I have been a working musician for most of my life. I've been married to the same woman for over 30 years. I am a college professor and I try to be a blessing unto this world in some small measure every day. Sometimes I get on my wife's nerves but as far as I know I cause no chaos in the world. I stir up no feelings of fear in anyone. Lord knows I'm not made of stone.

I disappoint myself.

Fuck You

In this 21st century global society in which we live, where our thoughts are transmitted around the world seconds after our brains process them and where every human being is connected to every other human being, little regard is given to aging and the aged. One is useless if not young, beautiful and in-style. There is an all-pervasive paranoia among those born after 1980 that sickens me: you must be on the cutting edge of cool.

If you have such a thought, you will NEVER be cool.

Who fucking cares what the trendsetters think? Who cares what the popular bitch in high school does? Why are you basing your life on the thoughts, words and actions of some 16-year-old future whore bimbo pig? Why are you giving credence to the ramblings of some soulless art critic or the artless advertising fools who create those fucking mind-numbing TV commercials or those brainless TV show hosts? Why are you allowing these people to run your lives? Are you that shallow?

I was an idiot like you once. I was plagued by feelings of insecurity. I was plagued with worries:

What if this record company asshole doesn't like my work?

What if that uncreative, conceited, follow-the-leader piece of shit bass player doesn't approve of the way I play bass?

Good God, what a way to live. It took me 30 years to realize that the only opinions of me that matter are The Lord's and my own. If you don't like my clothes, or my music, or this book, then fuck you. I don't care. My life was almost ruined by fear and anxiety because I gave up being a mobster, an outcast who loved being an outcast, in order to step in time to the rhythm tapped out by someone else. I wasted 30 years of mob life in order to kiss the ass of some suit just so I could pay my bills. I don't know how many times my father had to bail me out of financial binds. Instead of commanding fear and respect from these dick-less shit heads, I feared them. They held the purse strings. Instead of crushing their fucking skulls with my boot heels, I shook their sweaty little hands and thanked them for deeming to give me another gig to play or another record to produce.

What these 21st century scumbags don't understand is that age matters. With age comes experience, wisdom, and soul. One's life begins to make sense and the path is clear. It becomes impossible to ignore the joy that a warm breeze brings as it brushes your face. It becomes impossible to ignore the urge to savor every moment as if it was your last on earth. It becomes impossible to feel anything but sorrow for the 21st century scumbags who think they have all the answers at age 20. If you are the future, we are all screwed.

Hey little scumbag: you think you know everything, but you don't know anything.

I am a Baby Boomer. I don't mean to sound like a cranky old geezer, truly. I mean to sound like a pissed off mobster-turned-respectable-member-of-society-turned-mobster-again. I grew up in a simpler time. There were no cell phones or computers, although I think such gadgets are good things. It's the fuck-brains that use them for stupid reasons that I hate: Generation X jetsetters and the Millennial trendsetters. My abhorrence, detestation, revulsion, and disgust for you are boundless, you rat bastards. You have ruined the earth, killed chivalry and taken conceit and selfishness to new heights.

There are a good many people who fall into the age parameters of the Generation X set and the Millennial set. They are the hard working, level headed, respectful and down-to-earth people who are usually forgotten, trod upon, shat upon and who pay their taxes. These folks have my admiration. On their behalf, as well as for all the downtrodden and meek, and for my own interests, I submit the following:

I have spent far too many years obeying the rules of this shallow society. To every suit, superstar, trendsetter, and jetsetter: Fuck You.

We're All Weird

My late mother-in-law, God rest her sweet soul, was a very cool woman. She was one of the hippest people I ever met. One of the last things she said to me before she passed was, "We're all weird." That's a heavy statement. It can mean whatever you want it to mean. But I took it to mean that we're all different and that's OK. It reminds me of the Bible quote:

"Judge not, before you judge yourself." **(Matthew 7:1)**

It kind of puts us all in the same bag. Whether you're a Wall Street broker or a streetwalker, a *puttana*, you do what you have to do to survive. I grew up around violence. It was natural. It was so natural that I really didn't see anything wrong with attacking anyone who pissed me off. Some folks see that as wrong. But for me it was all I knew. Wall Street guys kill people, only they do it with money. They are the same as *puttanas.* They fuck you for a living. I am not judging them. One of my favorite quotes about judging people is by the late filmmaker Ed Wood: "I never judge my friends. If I did, I wouldn't have any." That's brilliant. It's a shame that most people never open themselves up to life. There is a lot of good shit out there waiting for you when you free yourself from the bondage of guilt, fear, greed and pride.

Mob guys are like any other people who live outside of the norm. Musicians, artists, hobos, hippies, Rastafarians and many other folks who are all classified as "weird" belong to this colony of outcasts. I see kids being swept up by the fatal winds of success at an early age. They live in a fantasyland. They are as weird as the craziest thug. Ultimately, we follow the path onto which we have been born. We share the common purpose: to fulfill our destinies. Those destinies might not be what the majority of people see as vital, useful or normal, but they are nonetheless our own. I suppose I might be considered weird for putting mobsters, musicians and Wall Street guys in the same group. But I don't see a difference. No matter what you do, you're always going to bring happiness, sadness, angst, emptiness and fulfillment to just about everyone in your life. Someone might be in your life for five minutes but you're going to impact that person on some level.

These are simply some thoughts on weirdness. We are who we are. Rarely if ever do we change much throughout our lives. I believe our lives follow a path much like an arc, as a boomerang cuts its circular path through the air. Ultimately, we end up where we began, perhaps a bit wiser, definitely battle-weary and scarred, but pretty much the same as we began: *Weird.*

Words

Words cut like knives, deep and painful. They puncture your faith like the fangs of a viper. You bleed tears. Your *Episodic Acute Stress* kicks in. You become filled with rage. Nothing worthwhile can happen. You are cornered. You growl like a mad dog. Everything that keeps you within the little box of civility that society has invented abandons you. You revert. You are again a wild beast.

Mobsters have feelings too. Mobsters cry. I've seen Patsy cry. Italians cry easily. We had a guy in the crew, Baldy. He cried like a baby when his daughter received her first Holy Communion, even when she'd say, "I love you, Daddy." He just broke down and wept. But they were tears of joy. When a mobster cries tears of sadness, whether figuratively or literally, somebody is going to die. You can count on it. Once you have developed a taste for blood, you have reverted and you can never come back. As I write these memoirs, so many decades after the fact, my taste for blood is as strong as ever. I enjoy watching people die. Fuck them. To this day, I don't care. I live within that little box of civility, but I would have no problem gutting someone like a deer if pushed too far, if the words spoken to me cut too deeply. I'm an emotional guy. Here is my mantra now:

War Is Hell: Have A Nice Day.

One time we were at our club, *The Little Shop of Insanity*, when a guy named Bruno walked in to see if there was anything interesting afoot. Bruno was a nice guy but he had a big mouth. He didn't mean to hurt your feelings. He just couldn't help himself. He said what was on his mind. He had no internal editor. Even mobsters, especially mobsters, have to have internal editors or they'd kill each other until there was no one left. Bruno would always say, "I mean no disrespect to you," if he saw his words had gotten on your nerves.

Most of the time, people let it go. *That stupid fuck Bruno isn't a bad guy. He has a big mouth. Forget about it.* But, Bruno apparently said something to the wife of one of the capos at a dinner party a few nights earlier. Buddy was as mean as a rattlesnake. He was a great guy most of time. But he was super sensitive. If you insulted him or if your words were perceived as an insult, it pretty much was a death warrant. I don't know what Bruno said to Buddy's wife. It was probably something like, "You look ravishing in that dress." He was probably staring at her boobs when he said it. Anyway, it bothered Buddy's wife so much that she told Buddy. By the time Bruno and Buddy were finally in the same room again, some three days later, the story had been blown way out of proportion. Bruno walked into *The Little Shop of Insanity* and Buddy was sitting at the table playing *Briscola* (the Italian card game) with my dad, Fat Patsy and me. Bruno was utterly unaware that he had insulted Buddy's wife, and thereby Buddy, as he entered the room. Bruno was about to greet everyone. He was in the middle of the word *Buongiorno* (an Italian greeting) but all Bruno got out was, *"Buongi..."* Buddy had a pistol with a silencer lying on the table. He picked it up so quickly I didn't even see him do it. All I remember is looking at my cards, hearing POP and hearing a thud. Gunshots didn't even startle me anymore. I glanced over and there was Bruno with a neat little bullet hole right between his eyes. The entire back of his skull was splattered on the front wall of the club. Bruno wasn't the first guy to have his brains blown out there. As I was staring at Bruno's twitching body, watching him die, I heard my dad say, *"Pssst."* I looked up and he said, "Can we get back to the game, please?" Ice water. Those crazy motherfuckers had antifreeze in their veins. Now I have antifreeze in my veins.

In this life you have to be careful that you don't hurt anyone's feelings. Today, you will upset people if you say some harmless thing such as, *"I think you look great in that sweater*." They'll take you to court for any little such misdemeanor you might unintentionally commit. *Yuppie bullshit.* Back in the day, their brains would be part of the wallpaper while they were still standing. Words can bring joy and encouragement into a person's life. They can fill your heart with love and they can cheer you up. But they can also hurt. They can rip into your soul until your spirit cries invisible tears. Sometimes people live their entire lives taking bullshit from others. When they die, they die knowing that they did the civilized thing. They ate shit and did nothing. At their funerals, people will say:

"What a sweet guy he was. He was never rude to anyone, he had such a forgiving heart." Fucking chump.

I have reverted back to that sick motherfucker I once was. I live in a *Little Shop of Insanity* of my own. I fought my way out of that place, lived in the civilized world for a lot of years, followed the rules and was careful to be a good person. But the years of inconsiderate scumbags who walk around in suits and carry briefcases have worn me down. They get away with saying rude things to people, hurting their feelings, and leaving a scene of devastation as real as Bruno's brains on the wall.

I have reverted.

I am an animal again.

Epilogue

(PATER MEUS, VIR MEUS)

Alphonse "Vegas" Moretti, a close friend of mine, asked me recently where I got the coglione ("balls" in Italian) to write this book. Its publication would reveal secrets kept under the lock and key of a blood oath over a century old. My answer was, "Vegas, if these guys were still alive I'd be in deep shit but they're all dead." Well, most are. My dad is still with us, albeit barely. The same holds true for Zoot. At this point, they don't care anymore. Unfortunately, they can't. Alzheimer's is a brutal disease. It wipes the memory clean. God only knows where Pop and Zoot are, psychologically, at this moment. But Dad still possesses that eerily magical capacity to speak to me with his mind. As he lies in his hospital bed unable to move, I can hear his voice clear as a bell. He has been able to do this since my childhood. When we played *Briscola*, the Italian card game, my dad would tell me what cards to play simply by looking at me, expressionless. I would look into his eyes and hear his voice, *Throw The Bullet*. I would slam my Ace of Diamonds down upon the table. Dad would jump to his feet, his chair flying backwards, and hammer a trump card onto to the table. *"Vaffanculo!" (Go Fuck Yourself!)* Patsy, Uncle Zoot, Dad and I would fall to the floor in hysterics. Big fun.

Al Vegas has witnessed this phenomenon first hand. On visits to the nursing home, he has seen my dad sit unmoving, peering out the window. Then, out of the blue, Dad would turn and look directly at me. Without words, simply by the look in his eye, I knew he wanted a glass of wine. Wine is forbidden at the nursing home but I always brought some anyway. I'm not about to tell a *Don*, "No." I would pour a few drops of his favorite Chianti into a shot glass and put it to his lips. Down the hatch the wine would go. Al Vegas asked:

"How in hell did you know he wanted a drink?" I don't know how I knew, I just knew.

Pop has possessed the ability to speak to me without words for as long as I can remember. When I was a kid, Pop would look at me from across the dinner table and I knew he wanted me to come up with some bullshit excuse to get him out of the house:

"Hey, Pop, would you take me to my band practice at the club?"

My father would say, *"Jeez, I promised your mother I'd stay home tonight."*

Mom would say, *"Oh, Domenico, take your son to band practice so he doesn't have to carry all that equipment."*

Pop would reluctantly agree and off we'd go. *"Thanks, boy, I'm proud of you,"* Pop would say. We'd hang out at the club, watch the ballgame, and play cards.

As I write this book, I hear his voice, dictating lines, reminding me to include this story and that story. I hear him suffering in his broken body. I know that within some deep, dark recess of his mind he is aware and communicating. I know he is not happy. I know that, at times, he wants to die. He doesn't speak coherently anymore. He doesn't make sense anymore with his vocal voice. But with his inner voice, the voice that cannot die, the voice that connects us, I hear him loud and clear. I don't know how much longer my father will last. For all he has been through, he has beaten the odds thus far and lives on. He is still fighting hard, much to the doctors' amazement. But even *Don Ventura* cannot live forever. We do not, unfortunately, travel in circular time. We do not live forever. Each day he becomes weaker. There have been three or four close calls in the past year. He was close to death each time. But each time, I heard Pop say to me, *"Not yet."*

As I got older, I had opportunities to “hit” people. While my assigned hits were, for one reason or another, aborted at the last minute, I was more than prepared to pull the trigger for Dad. I would do it now, happily. I have lost respect for my neighbor. I have tried to live within their wait-in-line society. It’s not for me. I have allowed far too many “respectable” people speak to me disrespectfully. I have done “the right thing” far too many times. It has gotten me a heart condition and grey hair, nothing more. I hear my father speak to me at this moment:

“Take shit from no one.”

So I have become unwavering in my resolve to live, finally, on my own terms. I don’t care. There are no tough guys left to test me. The true gangsters, except for Dad and Uncle Zoot, are all dead. I walk the streets looking for trouble, just as I did when I was 15 years old, Bowie knife at my side. It’s a different world. I could skin any of these so-called bad boys before they would ever know they were in a fight. I am so fucking sick of this lopsided world, where the rich get richer and the poor get poorer. They called us thieves! Holy fucking shit! So I roam the streets looking for the self-righteous, pompous, corporate, holier-than-thou, inconsiderate, pieces of shit who tortured me for decades. The day will come and when it does, there will be no end. I will come, raging, to find them and hell will come with me. I will laugh as I kick these bastards and bitches into the abyss.

I hear my father speak to me, *“Paura di nessuno.” (Fear no one.)*

I am my father’s son.

Pater Meus, Vir Meus: My Father, My Hero

Signed,

Trouble Ventura

THE END

Afterward

(Don't Worry About It)

In writing this book, I tried to incorporate the best parts of my real father's legacy: his generosity, his willingness to forgive, his quick wit, his street wisdom and his easygoing "don't worry about it" style. He continues to light the way for me, and he helps me stay focused on the most important things in life: love and happiness. He has been a blessing to me. He has shared his own blessings with me for my entire life. I hear his wonderfully "can do" adages in my mind all the time: "To try is to fail, do it!" and "The impossible takes a little longer." I pass these maxims to all who come to me for help, advice and comfort. My dad is truly my hero.

Thank you, Pop. I love you.

Joe Ferry

January 22, 2012

15500632R00104

Made in the USA
Lexington, KY
31 May 2012